Surrender to the Moonlight

Dria Andersen

To my husband, who was my sounding board, my cheerleader, my critique partner, and all the things I needed to finish this project. I appreciate every hour, every word of input, and most of all, your unwavering support.

To my family, who had to deal with mommy being on in another world for hours at a time. Thank you for your patience.

To my sister Tina, who reads everything I write and gives me honest feedback and encouragement, thank you mucho mucho. I appreciate your continued support and cheerleading! To my aunt Cathy who gave me my first love of romance stories, I thank you for allowing me to raid your bookshelf.

Thank you to every fan who continues to stick with me while telling the stories playing in my head. I appreciate each and every one of you. Also, I would like to give a special thanks to Pikko House for the feedback and help I get from your aloha readers.

Author's Note

My note for this story will be short. I am excited to start this series for a number of reasons. One: I feel like I'm starting to lean into my author voice, that's most important. Two: In my head as I was writing this, I was picturing how it would look as a TV show. I know on social media sometimes we say, 'oh, I would love to see a show like this...' and this series is that for me. I wrote it in a fictional town, but it's a town just like the one I grew up in. (Minus the supernatural creatures, of course.) I wanted the world to be country as hell, and fun and I hope I bring that out as you read the story.

And lastly, I'm really proud that I was able to finish this book. The pandemic has really shown me how ill-equipped I was to handle the steady stream of anxiety that the news and social media has been heaping onto us. I lost myself for a while there, but luckily for me, romance novels have been a saving grace of escapism and helped me to keep doing what I love. I only say that to just remind you, please take care of yourself and I hope my story brings you some kind of escape and joy in the midst of all of this.

Chapter One

"Mama used to always say, not everybody who is family is rooting for you."

"Oh Lord, not this again, mama. TiTi apologized." Nicole pushed her knee down on her suitcase and worked on zipping it.

The practical thing to do would be to take the clothes out and fold them properly, but she wasn't in the mood, so...she leaned harder on the top of the suitcase, grunting in victory when it zipped.

"And a lie don't care who tell it. She said that too," Lauren's accent was thick, betraying her aggravation.

On a regular day, her mother melded well into the urbanites in Connecticut, where she'd finally settled to be closer to her new husband's family. Her Georgia accent would be firmly tucked away, the clipped tones of New England helping her fit right in with her peers. Lauren could never pull it off when she was irritated, though, especially when talking to or about her family.

"Father God," Nicole whispered under her breath. Her mother was so damn dramatic.

She took a look around the hotel room to make sure she wasn't leaving anything behind. It was a mid-level hotel room, the same any government employee would use when traveling for work. It had two queen beds, a small desk in front of the bed, and a small sitting area off to the side, so there wasn't a lot of room for her to lose her stuff. All the same, she took a lap around it, leaning for a peek under the desk and armchairs.

"According to the lawyer, she divided it between her three grand-daughters. Equally, I might add. Aunt Shelby said they only cleaned the place up. She has no intention of keeping everything." Nic said as she kneeled between the beds.

"Shelby still stole mama's jewelry before I could even look through it."

Nicole imagined her mother on the other end of the call pouting. Lauren and her sisters had constantly been fighting for her grand-mother's attention. In light of Grandmother Patsy's death, now there was only 'stuff' to argue over. She closed her eyes and wondered how long she'd be subjected to her mother's current tirade. Finding the beds clear, she sat on the edge of the one she'd used to hold her clothes before she'd packed them.

"Perhaps if you'd spent more than an hour there after Grand-mother's funeral, you could've got what you wanted yourself," she muttered under her breath.

"Watch your mouth."

Nicole rolled her eyes. "Either way, I'm going, mama." She had to. Even being on the road was no longer helping. She was restless.

"I don't see why you want to go down there and get mixed up with all of mama's mess. What can you do that the police can't?"

"I'm not..." Nicole swallowed the growl building in her throat and stood to pace. Her mother always managed to get under her skin. "I'm going down there because the lawyer requested the three of us to come. Plus, it's been so long since I've been to Georgia for more than a day. Is it so bad that I want to pay my grandmother her last respects? It's already bad enough you kept her funeral from me."

"Excuse me for trying to protect my only daughter. I left to break the cycle. Why would you go back and stir it all up?"

She sucked her teeth, "Speaking of cycle, how is Gerard?"

Lauren sucked in a sharp breath, and Nicole immediately felt horrible for the dig. According to her grandmother, no Fouche could escape the family curse. It didn't stop her mother from trying. What was this, husband number four, five? Nicole shook her head.

"I'm sorry, mama, that was unnecessary."

Her mother sniffed. "Gerard is fine by the way, his children visit, with grandchildren. We've been enjoying it."

Nicole growled at that dig and decided she was done talking to her mother for the day. "Anyways, I'm already in Texas. It will take nothing for me to get to Grandmother's. I can relax there for a few weeks while I decide what to do with my share of the inheritance."

"Weeks! You barely visit me, and when you do, you go rushing off on assignment."

"Not you acting surprised we can't be in the same house for more than a few days at a time," Nicole muttered.

"Excuse your damn tone. I'm still your mother." Lauren snapped.

Nicole took a deep breath and sat down on her closed suitcase. Only on the phone for half an hour, and she and her mother were at each other's throats.

"I'm going to set up my office from there, so technically, I'm still working." She put on the cajoling tone she knew would calm Lauren's ire.

Lauren was silent for a tense moment. "Fine. Not like I could ever stop you from doing anything. You were always such—"

She growled, "Mama, please. You're pissed, got it."

Lauren huffed and took a deep breath. "Will you even call me when you arrive?"

Aah, and there was that new Yankee accent in place. It irritated Nicole that her mother changed herself for every new man in her life.

"Will the conversation be like this?" She shot back.

Lauren sucked her teeth. "Lord have mercy, goodbye."

"Love you, mama."

"So you say."

Lauren hung up, and Nicole counted that as a positive interaction. There were so many others that ended much worse, so she'd take what she could. Nicole peeked at the paperwork sitting on the hotel T.V. stand and chewed her bottom lip. How had the lawyer found her? She'd been all across east Texas for two weeks now documenting flood damage, the hotel room merely a pit stop in between locations. The bulky envelope had been waiting for her at the front desk when she'd come back from taking pictures. It had been surprising and timely. It felt like a sign to her. She could go to Georgia, do a couple of assignments while staying at her grandmother's place. See how it felt.

Her phone rang, and she blew out a breath when she realized who it was. She picked it back up.

"How did she take it?"

Nicole sucked her teeth but relaxed her shoulders. "A lot better than we suspected."

Her father snorted. "So she didn't accuse you of betraying her?"

"Close." She laughed. "Of course, she brought up Aunt Shelby and once again accused her of using her proximity to grandmother to steal her inheritance."

"The inheritance she didn't want?" Isaiah asked dryly.

Nicole sighed. "Let's not let facts get in the way. Besides, Aunt Shelby called me and apologized, said she didn't know mom wanted anything of grandmother's. She offered to send her all the pieces she wants."

"But Lauren would rather hold on to the mad?"

"Dad." She scolded as she dragged her suitcase off the bed and popped up the handle.

"I'm sorry, I didn't call to bad mouth your mother. I just want you to be careful. Someone murdered your grandmother."

"I need to do this, dad." She was starting to question if it was worth all the fuss.

He sighed and was silent. Nicole didn't bother filling it, she knew how her father was.

"Your grandmother was a practitioner, Bean. Do you know what kind of magic users or supernaturals live there? Have you checked?"

"I hadn't even thought of it, to be honest, dad. But, there are supernaturals all over this country. It's not any more dangerous than the city I've been working out of for the past two weeks."

He did make a good point. Nic should probably look into that. Would an internet search of the town bring up anything? Did City Hall keep records? She eyed the package from her grandmother's estate. Would they have that type of information in there?

He sighed again. "Fine, call me when you get there."

"I will. Love you."

"Love you too, Bean."

She snorted and ended the call. She looked around at her hotel room. Everything was packed. All she needed to do was load it all into her SUV. With some mental gymnastics, she could count the whole thing as an adventure, no different than all the others before it. It was not like she expected to solve a murder in two weeks.

Chapter Two

If Nicole took the time to examine why what was supposed to be a sixteen-hour drive turned into three days, she'd have to admit to dreading this trip. She'd done the song and dance for her parents about how excited she was, but with every mile closer she'd come to Springbrook, anxiety was taking over. What if her mother had been right? What if she stirred up the curse talk to the detriment of her family? It wasn't as if the time was wasted, she'd found a few small towns along the way that had the back of her SUV filled with trinkets and books she'd found in the local thrift stores. She couldn't wait to dive in and assess what she'd seen. So...all in all, stalling hadn't been a bad idea.

Well, that stalling hadn't been. The current stalling she was doing—sitting in her jeep in her grandmother's yard staring at Patsy's memory-laden house— not so much.

It was dark outside, but the modern touches her grandmother had added to the place were evident. It was the same sprawling farmhouse, four different size roof pitches, contrasting window shutters, all of that familiar, just a fresh coat of paint and landscaping that had her eyes stinging. Patsy had loved gardening, and it showed in her front yard. It was something the two of them had in common.

"I'll keep your babies alive, grandmother," Nicole said quietly.

A breeze shook the jeep, and she shuddered. *Time to go in.* She got out of the car and shivered in the dark air. Springbrook itself technically was a town. There was what her grandmother called a 'minute mart,' a post office, but not much else. Street lights included. The Fouches lived far enough outside of the city that it could no longer be called the outskirts. The land Patsy's house sat on had been passed down through generations of Fouches split between all the siblings. She had all manner of family in either direction she turned, mere acres separating them from each other. It had been idyllic when she was a kid. Cousins, first through third, were steps away. Summers had been heaven.

She looked forward to reacquainting herself with them.

Nicole pulled out the envelope the lawyer had sent, using the key inside to open the front door. She was once again surprised by the décor. Patsy had wholly changed everything inside. Gone was the chintzy, flowery furniture, and in its place were modern, lush pieces. The front door opened up to a small foyer, right in front of the living room. The original wooden floors spanned the hallway and led right to the wide staircase. Left of that stairway would be the kitchen. She was excited to see what her grandmother had done there. It had been one of Patsy's favorite places. She smiled. Her grandmother had been happy to tell her about the changes she'd made when they talked on the phone. It pleased Nicole how well it had all come together. She was happy to be home. Though it had been a lot of years since she'd been back, the house seemed to embrace her.

She wiped away a happy tear.

When was the last time she'd been back? Lauren had divorced her second husband and decided that she wanted no parts of Georgia. Nicole hadn't been allowed to come back any more summers. Instead, she traveled with her mother while Lauren decided which state suited her best. They'd eventually settled in Virginia for a few years that time. It was one of the longer places they'd stayed. That nomad life had stuck with her, given her own career choice. But, as she wheeled her suitcase down the hallway upstairs to find a room, Patsy's spirit seemed to wrap around her and welcome her. If she had to settle somewhere, here wouldn't be a bad place to do it.

Hours later, done unpacking and exploring, Nic sent off quick text messages to her parents to let them know she'd arrived safely. She also sent ones to Vanessa and Audrey, the two cousins she shared her inheritance with. They'd be coming in in the next couple of days, so she would enjoy the house to herself for as long as she could. She fixed a sandwich for dinner, surprised and pleased to find the refrigerator stocked as well. She knew Aunt Shelby was the one to thank for that. She'd walk over to her house tomorrow and thank her in person.

She wandered back into the office she'd found, curious about what she would find. Her grandmother's desk was neat and organized. There was a computer, but that wasn't surprising. Patsy wasn't a technophobe, but she did find having the machine daunting. She only used the tablet Nic had sent her a few years ago so they could video chat. The tablet was on top of a journal, which was a curious thing for Aunt Shelby to leave behind. They'd divvied up all Patsy's other belongings. Sliding the tablet to the side to explore later, she opened the journal. It felt odd reading her grandmother's words, but it also felt like she was close to her. She tilted her head at some of the entries. They were what looked like notes on beer-making methods. She stopped chewing. It was the recipe for her grandmother's company's beer. She flipped through and saw more annotations and names of people she'd given to try her beer. She was awed by the information. It was all about the start of Patsy's company and the many hurdles she'd gone through to start it. There was a guy who appeared a lot, named JT. He'd helped her grandmother perfect her first recipe and was even the first customer for the company.

His bar was local; maybe she could visit the bar tonight. It was only a little after 9 p.m. surely a bar, even in this small town, stayed open. She closed the journal and stood, stretching her body. She went to the back door, and the woods seemed to call to her. She stepped outside and tilted her head towards the full moon. She worried her lip, dreading what was coming. It was the part of the curse she hated the most. She could never control it, though she was getting better about predicting when it would happen. The most she could hope for was that she didn't get into any trouble while she was in the body of the cougar. Would she be safe in these woods? As her body cracked and morphed without any input from her, she realized two things, one: she wasn't getting to that bar tonight, and two: maybe coming back to where her family was cursed had not been a good idea.

Chapter Three

There were downsides to living in a small town, especially where you grew up. For one, everyone knew your business, and two, they weren't shy about spreading it around. Owning the only bar for thirty miles meant that it all eventually reached his ears. In JT's line of work, that was one of the top benefits of small-town life. His work didn't precisely align with local law, and knowing the movements of the town's residents had saved him a time or three in the past.

Take now, for instance. JT had barely been behind the bar five minutes before the newest rumors reached him. This time of day, the local retirees were the only patrons in his bar. They came in for a lunchtime beer, town gossip, and sometimes a game or two of pool or darts. Usually, he was in the back, handling paperwork, but today, he was waiting on those rumors to reach him.

Somebody had killed a local practitioner in his territory, and JT had every intention of finding out who the hell had been so bold.

"Amber out?" Mike was a regular, and what he didn't know, he could always find out. At least, let him tell it.

"The baby's feeling sick," JT answered, pouring Mike his favorite beer without being prompted.

The older man smiled in appreciation before leaning forward, his face straightening. "There were lights on at Patsy's last night."

He paused what he was doing. "Did you check it out?"

"Ain't my business, I just happen to be walking through," the old man said. "I heard the granddaughters were moving in for a while until Patsy's affairs are settled."

"Hmm," was all JT said as he slid the beer over to him.

He knew Mike wouldn't need prodding if he had information to pass along. He served another patron and waited him out. He briefly wondered if the granddaughters moving in would impact him at all. It wouldn't stop him from searching out the person or persons who'd killed their grandmother, but there was nothing saying the women wouldn't get in his way. For all he knew, they were satisfied with the answers the police had given the family.

"Shame what happened to Patsy. She was good people." Mike said, finally.

JT nodded. Patsy had been a favorite in this town. She'd helped a lot of people, and plenty of the town's residents were pissed about her murder. As far as the sheriff's department was concerned, a vagrant passing through town had tried to rob the old woman and killed her. If it was one thing JT avoided, it was the police. His pack moved all manner of illegal items across Georgia's border, so he did not get involved with the law.

Besides, he had no plans to turn the murderer over to them anyhow, so what they believed didn't matter to him at all.

Mike tapped the bar for a refill, and JT obliged him.

"Police still ain't looking for nobody," Mike grumbled. "But I can't imagine the Taylor pack will let it go."

JT grunted, not denying or confirming. Since he was alpha of the Taylor pack, it wouldn't be in his best interest to feed gossip. At least not at this time. Their reputation was well-earned, but for the most part, it was hearsay. Certainly nothing that could be repeated and accepted in a court of law.

He and Mike both turned towards the bar door when it opened. The woman who entered was no local. JT knew almost everyone in town, and he'd never seen her before, though he knew immediately the trouble she brought with her. Tight jeans, a mean look on her face, and those unmistakable eyes. The Fouche women all had those eyes. Their feline features and petite bodies were well known in the area. The beautiful women had a reputation for chewing up and spitting out men. It was taken as fact that they didn't keep a man once they'd taken their fill of him.

Something about her reached out to him, drew him in. His wolf sensed the power in her and sat forward in interest. Was she dangerous?

Maybe.

Would that stop him from trying to holla?

His eyes traced her body, swinging on the curve of her hip up to her full breasts...

Yeah, nope. It definitely wouldn't stop JT.

Mike turned to him and caught him staring. The old man whistled. "You wanna leave those Fouche women alone, son. That's a ride not everyone gets off alive."

JT smiled and set the man's drink down. "Every man ain't me," he said.

Mike chuckled and turned his body towards the bar to keep from staring. "Arrogance is a privilege of youth."

He swallowed down his laugh as the woman carefully climbed the bar stool. Her large eyes were tilted up on the ends, deep onyx and surrounded by lush lashes. She wore minimal makeup, though her full lips were shiny from some kind of gloss. His wolf sat up, very interested in the petite woman. Her scent reached him over every other smell in the bar. Even the wings his cook was slinging in the back. He closed his eyes and inhaled deeply. She gave him a grimace that he assumed was supposed to be a smile.

"Hi."

Lord help him; her voice was husky, almost hoarse. It put to mind long nights of making her scream his name.

He cleared his throat and nodded. "What can I get for you?"

"My name is Nicole, and my grandmother, Patsy, sold beer to you?" Though she posed it as a question, her tone was confident, no-nonsense.

He nodded, assessing her with an interest that was probably dangerous. At least, let the town tell it.

Her eyes moved around his bar, taking in everything and darting towards the exits before swinging back around to him. JT looked around and tried to view his bar from a newcomer's perspective. He supposed it didn't look like a traditional dive bar, but he took pride in his place. The exposed brick walls and dark wooden beams crossing the ceiling should've made the place look dark, but pendant lights shaped like bottles hung from the ceiling. The front windows were high enough to ensure privacy but also let the midmorning sunlight in to brighten the place.

"I'd like to try one, please." She ran her hand across the polished cement of his bar top.

He was surprised and reached back for a glass filling it up from the tap. He passed it over.

"Patsy made a good beer," Mike spoke up next to her.

She leaned down and inhaled. A smile spread across her face. "I can't believe my grandmother made this."

He leaned his elbows on the bar, his curiosity skyrocketing. "You didn't know?"

Her smile dimmed. "We talked about it, but this is my first time tasting it. I haven't been back to Georgia in a while."

Interesting.

That would explain why he didn't know her. "She's in a few bars from here to Jacksonville. I know Brandon was working on getting it stocked further north."

Her smile was sad. She lifted the glass to take a sip, and JT watched for her reaction. He cataloged all her facial movements, fascinated by her. Perhaps because she was new, shiny. His wolf said differently, but he wasn't going to worry about that. Her eyebrows shot up, and she took another sip.

"How is it?"

She let out a shaky laugh. "I like it."

"Good, right? Patsy was almost magic with it." He winked at her, and she looked startled. He swallowed a chuckle. "I'm JT."

He held out his hand, and she stared at it a moment before gripping it tightly. His wolf's power raised, his chest filling with energy as his animal got its first glimpse of the cat Nicole hid under her skin. Her magic brushed his, and JT understood instinctually that he was dealing with another predator. Now, just why did that intrigue him more?

He licked his lips and released her hand. "I own this place, so if you have any problems, let me know."

"Thank you. I just came for this." She held up the beer, her voice soft, breathless.

Had she felt the way her magic responded to his wolf?

"All the same," he said and left her to what looked like brooding.

He was familiar with the concept himself. His phone at his hip vibrated, and he slipped to the back before checking it. It was another cousin of his.

"Yeah."

"Loaded and ready when you are," Dante told him.

"Alright, we'll move it tonight." He hung up and stole another glance at Nicole.

She downed the rest of her beer, set down money on the bar, and left. Her graceful stride was hypnotizing. His wolf was urging him to do things that weren't smart. Like Mike said, not many men could escape the Fouche women in one piece. He had just enough reckless-ness in him that the challenge would be fun. According to his mother, he had a hard head and liked to do things the hard way. What Valerie

Taylor didn't understand was that sometimes, the hard way was the most fun.

Chapter Four

Hours later, JT got on his bike and headed to his parents' house. He made it a habit to see them before he made any runs. He smiled, seeing his little sister's Prius in their yard, parked haphazardly as usual. His parents didn't have a driveway, just patchy grass with a few worn spots where various family members parked on the regular. He parked his motorcycle on the side of his sister's car because he didn't trust her. He'd been a witness to her driving lessons, so it was better to be where she could see his bike.

He stomped his feet off on the porch, toeing off his boots inside the door. The whole house was an open floor plan, so he could spot his mother in the kitchen. Valerie looked up from the stove smiling, happy to see her firstborn. She wore a loose jumper and smelled of vanilla bean, her favorite soap. She'd tied her short hair down under a floral scarf, and her face was free of makeup, which meant she was in for the evening.

He kissed her on the cheek, peeking into the pot she'd been stirring. "What you making?"

"Nothing but a lil okra and tomato with some white rice."

That sounded perfect to him. He could have dinner with his parents and head out from here.

His mother settled into a chair at the well-used dining table in the kitchen. From the leafy pile of vegetables on the table, she'd been chopping greens.

"It's some venison in the smoke house from when me and daddy went running the other night," Valerie told him.

Oh snap, even better. "It's ready?"

"Should be," was her answer.

He looked towards the back of the house, where a hallway led to four bedrooms. "Jus here?"

"Came for the weekend to run a bit. You staying for dinner?"

He nodded.

His mama turned towards the hall. "Justine, go outside and get me some Lima beans and a couple of cucumbers!" She yelled towards the back.

Shuffling feet preceded his sister. Justine was nearly as tall as JT, her body leggy, rangy like all the women on their mother's side of the family. She wore a romper that showed way too much of her caramel skin for his liking.

"I's free, Ms. Millie," Justine said in a mocking voice as she entered the kitchen.

Valerie sucked her teeth and pinched Justine's arm.

"Dang, mama, I'm just joking."

"Your narrow behind better joke with somebody else. I ain't one of your little friends," Valerie said.

JT snickered as Justine gave him a big hug. He was always happy to see his little sister. He missed her now that she was off in college. Her face was a clone of their mother's: high cheekbones, rounded nose, and large eyes. Where Valerie's eyes were sharp, aware of every-thing around her, Justine's dark eyes were open, friendly, but so mischievous.

She pulled back and met his eye, inclining her head towards the door. He caught the hint. "I'll help."

He grabbed his sister around the shoulder, grabbing the bowl his mother thrust at them. They walked in silence the few yards over to the garden his parents kept in their back yard. Justine took the bowl from him and bent down to gather the beans.

"What's up?"

"I ain't one to mind your business," she started.

He frowned at her. "Because your head should be in them books."

"I know, I know. I hear things, though." She propped the bowl on her hip.

"Jus, this ain't the life I want for you."

Justine rolled her eyes. "You making mad money. What if I want to do the same?"

"All money ain't good money."

She blew out a raspberry.

"Now, tell me what you got."

"I heard second or third hand, so you can't quote me on it, but the Wulfen are looking for shit to move down the interstate."

He crossed his arms over his chest. "What type of shit?"

He wasn't worried about drugs or guns moving through his territory. It wasn't his business, so long as they didn't stop in this town. They didn't deal in petty shit like that. The Taylors liked power, and there was nothing more powerful than magic.

"Ingredients firstly."

"For?"

She shrugged. "That's all I heard. But ain't but a few type of ingredients to be had along this side of the interstate, especially since the drug game is on lock."

JT cursed and pulled out his phone. He sent off some text messages to his crew and slid it back in his pocket. His sister was right. The marsh was ripe with hiding places where a knowledgeable person could grow certain ingredients that discerning practitioners and root workers needed. Some of it was impossible to grow in other areas, which worked perfectly for him.

"You gave it to me. Now let it be."

"I'm not looking for trouble, big brother. I just happened to stumble onto that bit of gossip."

He eyed his sister. It was true that he made a lot of money getting magical items that were hard to procure. Anything from books to antique relics others were too wary of moving, he couriered it all. It wasn't something he wanted his sister involved with. For one, the people he dealt with were a different breed...literally in most cases. If it were just witches, shifters, or practitioners... maybe he wouldn't mind, but other more dangerous things moved in the night. Most of them were unstable, all of them were dangerous.

"When you go back to Albany?" He changed the subject.

"Sunday, I just came for the weekend."

"You need anything?"

"I'm good, JT," she answered, picking the cucumbers.

He grunted and dropped it. They both knew he'd slide money into her car before he left.

He helped her pick the rest of the beans, and they walked back to the house in silence. Justine dropped the vegetablea on the table and turned to go back into her room.

"Aht aht, come shell them," Valerie ordered.

Jus sucked her teeth but sat down to do as ordered. He sat next to her and kissed her temple; he loved the brat. She swatted him away.

"Where's daddy?" JT asked, picking up a pod to help.

Valerie rolled her eyes. "Down to Earl's, supposedly he got a new boat."

"Uncle Earl got a boat?" Jus asked, surprised. "Auntie Cheryl let him buy it?"

"Let your auntie tell it, it ain't no bigger than that couch." Valerie nodded toward her favorite floral love seat.

Justine snickered. "Auntie Cheryl is such a hater. It's gotta be at least bigger than a sofa."

JT shook his head and grabbed more beans. "What he doing with it?" He asked out of curiosity. Access to a boat always came in handy out here in the marsh.

"Crabbing," his mother said with a shake of her head.

"Crabbing?" Jus repeated, outright laughing. "I'm going by there to see the size of this boat."

"Chile, your daddy, and Earl retired, and now we gotta deal with a hundred different hobbies," his mama muttered. "Both of 'em gettin' on my nerves."

He laughed because, despite her grumbling, her eyes were sparkling. She enjoyed having his father home and out of danger.

"Who these beans for?" He asked.

"Pastor appreciation tomorrow." She answered.

Jus rolled her eyes.

"Quit rolling your eyes at the Lord."

"It ain't the Lord I'm scoffing at," she shot back.

Their mother narrowed her eyes and then sucked her teeth. "Anyways. Why you ain't tell me Patsy's granddaughter was back in town." She directed that question to JT.

"Which one it is?" Justine asked.

"Nicole." He answered without thinking.

His sister smirked.

"Umm-hmm," Valerie said slyly. "Heard she came down to the bar."

"Well, if you heard everything, what you asking me for?" He grumbled.

"What you getting snippy for?" Valerie smiled.

"I'm not getting snippy. You probably know more from your daily game of telephone than I do, is all I'm saying."

"I don't remember them," his sister commented.

Valerie shrugged. "They left way before you were old enough to notice. Only one who came back regularly was Ness, with her crazy self. Love my Ness."

JT barely kept from rolling his eyes. His mother collected people like some women did shoes.

"Her mama the one told me they were all coming," Valerie said.

"All three of them?" JT asked, even though he knew the answer.

"Mmhmm."

"I know Ness, but what Nicole look like?" Justine asked.

He pulled up her features in his mind. Not that he'd be giving his mother fodder for the gossip tree. "Like every Fouche woman before her." He answered.

"Pretty little things," his mother said. "Every last one of them."

"Came by to taste Ms. Patsy's beer." He added.

"Hmm," was Valerie's response to that. "When the other two coming?"

"Mama, I don't know. I may have exchanged ten words with the woman."

"Why are they in town?" Justine asked.

His mother answered. "Patsy left everything to the three of them."

He perked up at that. "Everything?"

"I think Brandon is still in charge of the liquor business, but only as like an employee. She gave the company over to the girls."

"That I didn't know," JT said. He wondered if it would affect his inventory. That was the only reason he cared.

"We'll see how that goes," Valerie said.

JT dropped the subject and asked his sister about school. Since he was making a run, he wouldn't get a lot of time with her. He sat back and relaxed in the chair, letting the chatter of the two women rise and fall around him. He loved being home.

Chapter Five

Even after her impulsive lunch trip, Nicole was able to get a lot of work done. She'd clocked out having completed everything on her to-do list, but she carried her work phone with her as she got into the car headed to Westport's small jet port. Ness's flight would be arriving soon. She looked forward to seeing her cousin.

Once she pulled out of the dirt road that led to her family's land, she got onto the two-lane highway that would carry her there, admiring the tall trees that flanked it. It was a beautiful place, the marsh sporadically breaking up the forests. The tension she'd typically felt throughout the day was absent. Her shoulders relaxed every time her car bumped over a bridge. She'd already crossed two separate bridges over the small tributaries and rivers, fishers on the banks of both.

Her thoughts strayed to her lunchtime jaunt to Springbrook's only bar. It hadn't been impressive on the outside. Well, inside either. It was a hole in the wall, clean, but the motorcycles scattered around the gravel told the story of the patrons, so she shouldn't have expected anything fancy. For a town that small, she'd been shocked to find it at all. It looked and seemed to function as a clubhouse for a motorcycle gang. There had been customers scattered around the small tables, eating and playing pool, so maybe that wasn't its only function. She could also admit that the place had been a lot nicer than she had expected.

How in the world had her grandmother been involved? Her mind drifted to the bartender that had helped her.

JT.

Yeah, she'd be seeing those dark eyes in her dreams tonight. She had a weakness for dark skin men, and with his beard, full lips, and dark eyes, JT pushed all her buttons. Not even that he was just physically fine, the power coming off that man...whew Lord. Her magic had responded immediately, and the cat she battled on a daily basis had rushed forward to experience him. He had to be some type of shifter because she'd never reacted to a regular person like that...ever.

Her cat was a curious creature, and the moment her skin had touched JT, it was like a wildfire was set off in her body. She still felt flushed from the slight contact. Her cat wanted to play with him, and if Nicole hadn't come to town with a mission, she would've jumped on that immediately.

She shook her head and steered her thoughts back to the main reason she was back in Springbrook. Her grandmother's murder. Patsy had mentioned JT in her journal a few times. She'd noted that he'd tasted all her beer recipes before she'd established the company. She even mentioned some business they had together, though she hadn't gone into detail. At least not from what Nicole read.

How close were they?

Would he know anything about how Grandmother had died?

If her grandmother was involved with a motorcycle club, could that be a reason she had been murdered? It was something to explore later. Not that she was trying to give herself reasons to go back to his place. Or to see him, it was all a part of her investigation.

As she drove, trees gave way to small shopping centers until she stopped at the first red light in Westport. It let her know she'd crossed into 'town.' Her eyes widened at how much growth the small city had undertaken. There was actually a Target and a couple of big store chains. She followed her GPS directions to the jet port and parked. From the number of cars in the lot, the only people present were the staff. There was a small rental agency with about six cars, but that was really it. She went inside and waited. According to the text message Ness sent her last night, the estate had paid for her to fly directly into the small airport.

She was nervous, but at the same time, excited to see her cousin. It had been some years since they'd last been able to hang out. And even the time they'd had together after childhood had been spent playing referee between their respective mothers. How old had they been since they spent any significant amount of time together?

Years ago!

They'd both happened to be in the same city at the same time and had met for dinner. That had been at least five years ago. Nicole sighed at that. She frowned as she looked up. A woman across the way was staring. Nic gave her a wan smile she usually wouldn't have. Normally, she would turn her back, but they were in a small town; all these people knew each other. She could almost feel Grandma Patsy over her shoulder telling her not to be rude. Unfortunately, the woman proved why Nicole never smiled at people, because she came over. Nicole swallowed a sigh.

"You one of them Fouche girls?"

"Excuse me?"

"One of Patsy's," the woman's voice was matter of fact.

"Yes, Patsy was my grandmother," she answered reluctantly.

"Mmm-hmm, you got that Fouche look. Y'all some pretty little thangs. Ain't bigger than a minute," the woman eyed her up and down.

Nicole felt her temper rise, but she knew what that could bring, so she tamped down on it.

The woman continued with no input from Nicole. "I'm sorry for your loss."

"Thanks," she muttered and walked off.

Nic looked down at the linen jumper and the wedged sandals she wore to give her some height. *Not bigger than a minute.* She wanted to be offended, but she had to own that at five-five. She put her head down in her phone to avoid making eye contact with the many people staring. She should've expected it. The patrons of the hole-in-the-wall bar had done the same. For a local joint in a small town, it had been hopping.

Her mind went back to JT. She blew out an impatient breath. She didn't have time to be looking or even thinking about men. If only she could get her hormones on board. As it was, just the thought of JT had her rearranging her priorities. Sex didn't take that much time in the grand scheme of things. It wasn't as though she wanted to get serious with the man. But then, it was a small town, so avoiding him afterward could get tricky.

She blew out an impatient breath.

She needed to let it go. She would not let her cat's curiosity get them both into trouble.

There was some shuffling which she took to mean the plane was landing. There was no announcement, but the luggage cart off to her right started moving. Six or seven businessmen flooded into the terminal from a side door, and she smiled as she spotted the wide-brimmed hat that surely had to belong to her cousin. She stuck her phone back into her purse and waited as the men parted. Vanessa Fouche sashayed through in breezy wide-legged pants and a button-up tied under her ample breasts. Nicole certainly understood the staring as Ness made her way over to her. Her cousin was beautiful.

"Nic!" Vanessa called out before sweeping her into a hug.

"Ness," she breathed out as her cousin squeezed.

Tears obscured her vision for a moment as she soaked in the woman's presence. She hadn't realized how much she missed her. Yes, they made cursory calls and social media comments, but after having spent summers together, phone calls didn't hit the same. In her arms, it felt like no time had passed at all. There was no awkwardness.

Ness pulled back. "Jesus, you're gorgeous. I know I say it all the time, but really, cousin."

Nic wiped her face. "Chile, please, you."

Ness waved her off. "Let's get out of here."

"How many bags did you bring?" Nic looked towards the spinning luggage.

Ness shook her head. "I just have this carry-on. I got the rest of my stuff shipped."

Nicole raised an eyebrow in surprise. "Just like that?"

Ness studied her face. "Yeah, I...I'm going to take Grandmother's summons as fate."

They stared at each other, something passing between them that Nicole couldn't name. But she nodded because she understood. She'd told her mother that she was only staying for a couple of weeks, but really in her heart, she'd already decided.

"I haven't had a roommate since college," she commented, taking the small rolling suitcase from Ness's hand.

Ness snorted. "This'll be fun. If we decide to stay, we can grow old together, three cat ladies living in the woods."

Nicole snorted at how accurate that statement was.

Chapter Six

ess sighed next to her. "It's so damn beautiful here."

Nicole tapped on the steering wheel to the music and smiled. "Isn't it?"

"I needed this, Nic. I can't tell you how much."

Nicole nodded because she could understand. "I talked to Aunt Shelby this morning, and she wanted to see us. I can drop you and the car off at Grandmother's and walk by myself if you're too tired."

"I don't mind visiting."

Nicole nodded and pulled onto the dirt road that led to her grandmother's house. She could tell the exact moment she crossed back over Patsy's property line. It was as though the rest of the world fell away. Peace stole over her. Nic spared her cousin a glance as Ness sucked in a surprised breath. Ness's head was down, her hands covering her face. Nicole stopped the car and pulled her cousin into a hug.

"I know."

"We stayed away too long," Ness whispered.

Nic could only nod past the lump in her throat. She felt like they'd abandoned their grandmother. She wanted to be mad at her mother, but she was old enough to make her own decisions. She'd blamed it on being busy at work, traveling, but the truth was, she should've made time.

"We're here now," Nic soothed.

Ness nodded and pulled from her. She blew out a breath and pulled down the mirror. "Jesus, look at my face." She pulled something out of her purse and proceeded to fix her makeup.

Nic wiped her own face and put the car back in drive. They arrived and left Ness's suitcase in the car for later. They walked towards the woods that separated Patsy's house from her eldest daughter's. There was a foot path in the woods, worn from the many steps taken between the houses. The route diverted into two other directions, one leading to her Uncle Brandon's house and the other to the property divided between Patsy's other daughters. Though, that plot of land stood empty since they'd scattered.

She frowned at how worn the path was. It meant there had been a lot of traffic. There was only one house still standing, the one Audrey's mother lived in once upon a time. The trailers Nicole and Vanessa had grown up in had long been moved and junked. Would Aunt Kit's house still be standing? She made a note to check it later. They carried on to their Aunt Shelby. The path cleared, and the two-story craftsman that was her aunt's house loomed ahead of them. Immediately Nicole was transported back to her childhood and how she and her cousins raced through the path to eat at Aunt Shelby's. Shelby would be on her porch in a wide-brimmed straw hat and a white house dress, rocking, sipping what Nicole knew was the best lemonade she'd ever tasted.

"TiTi!" Ness yelled and waved.

It pulled Nicole from her memories. Her aunt smiled wide and stood from her chair. Approaching sixty, her aunt was beautiful, leaning gracefully into her age. Her coarse hair was white, pulled into a low ponytail that trailed her back. Her signature wide-legged culottes and tank top pressed neatly. Her aunt was fit, muscular from what her cousin Cellus called 'momma's fast ass gallivanting.' She smiled at the thought of her aunt in the gym taking classes and hanging out with hunky younger men.

"There go my girls," Shelby said happily.

Her aunt swept them up in hugs. Aunt Shelby cupped Nic's cheeks and smiled. "So beautiful. Come sit."

They both grabbed a chair and a glass of lemonade. Nicole closed her eyes as the tart taste exploded on her tongue. It brought back so many memories. Her aunt used to leave a giant water cooler jug full of it on her porch for them as they played outside.

"I'm so glad you girls are here," Shelby broke into her thoughts.

"It came at the best possible time," Nic said. "I'm sorry I didn't make it to the funeral."

Nicole swallowed down her guilt. She'd found out about the funeral from her mother, but only after the fact. Lauren had attended 'on both their behalves', and Nicole had been furious. Would her mother have told her about the funeral if she hadn't received the summons from her grandmother's estate? Shelby touched her shoulder.

"Stop, Nicole. Everybody there heard Lauren fussing and rushing every damn thing," her aunt soothed. "She ain't hide the fact that she didn't tell you about it."

"I can't believe I missed it," Nic said.

"I'm sorry I didn't reach out to you about it. I just assumed Aunt Lauren would've told you," Ness said.

"Alright, no more talking about my mama," Nic pleaded. She would deal with that in her own time.

"Aunt Lauren was very vocal about not staying," Ness added anyway.

"Yeah, she didn't want to chance the curse rubbing off and getting on her new marriage," Shelby said, sipping from her lemonade.

An awkward silence dropped between them.

Until...

"Girl, what number this is?" Ness asked.

She snickered and cleared the lump from her throat. "Four...wait, five, I think actually. I keep getting them mixed up."

Shelby sighed. "Well, you can't say my sister ain't trying."

Nic smiled, shook her head, and searched for something to steer the conversation away from Lauren and her disastrous track record.

Ness took care of that. "Has the police said anything?"

It was the same question she had though Nic had thought to ease into asking. The thing about her cousin Vanessa was that she never eased into anything. The forthright child had grown into a woman equally blunt and plain-spoken. Nic held her breath for the answer.

Shelby sighed. "Not a damn thing. We ain't heard hide nor hair from any of them. I would be surprised if they were even trying."

Nicole shook her head in aggravation, and a renewed sense of purpose washed over her. "What all do you know?"

Her aunt shrugged. "I had no clue mama was even worried about something. The night it happened, I heard her call my name, and I woke up out of a dead sleep and knew she was gone."

Ness grabbed her aunt's hand. "And no one knows nothing?"

"No one around here would touch mama. Y'all know that."

Nicole nodded because Patsy was well known and well-loved in these parts. It made her death even more shocking because of it.

"Why did they settle on robbery?" She would definitely need more information. Perhaps she could go down to the station herself.

"According to them and the 'evidence,' mama came in on a robbery, and the person hit her in the head with one of her statues and ran off," Shelby said tiredly.

"Will they share the evidence?" Nicole asked.

Ness gave her a sharp look.

"Cellus is looking into it. He won't drop it." Shelby refilled her glass. "I just don't have the spoons to deal with it."

"That's understandable," Ness soothed.

Nicole pulled out her phone and texted her cousin. If Cellus had information, she wanted access to it. She looked up, and her heart squeezed at her aunt's face. She was grieving heavily. Aunt Shelby and Grandmother Patsy were very close.

"I chat with Cellus all the time, but how is Damian and the new baby?" She changed the subject.

Shelby lit up. "Hold on, I got some pictures on my phone. Marcellus tagged me in them on Facebook."

Ness cackled, "oh lord, not you on the internet, TiTi. You been on them dating sites looking at men?"

"Nah, Cellus said she in the gym picking up young bucks," Nic joked.

Shelby busted out laughing. "Don't be getting fresh with me. My business is my own. My son talk too much."

Nic cackled.

"I knew it!" Ness snickered.

"Whatever." Shelby pulled her glasses up from around her neck and scrolled through her phone. "Look at my grandbabies," she passed them the phone.

Nic smiled and cooed respectfully at the picture of Damian's three kids and his wife. They looked so happy. It was almost unfair how the men avoided the Fouche curse.

"Damian actually works for the Brewery, right?" She asked to distract herself from that depressing thought. "How did he take it with Grandmother leaving it to us?"

"Mmhmm. Mama had him coming up with flavors and stuff. Don't worry about your cousins. They are exactly where they want to be. Mama made sure to check with them." Aunt Shelby said, putting her phone down on the table.

That surprised her. "So she told y'all what she was doing?"

"Not me, the boys. Called them over there to dinner one night a few months ago. Julian told me after the funeral." Shelby answered.

Nic frowned. "Was it something she always planned?"

Shelby gave a sad sigh. "You know, I don't all the way know. I thought, I mean, I knew she was gonna give y'all the house and some land. She gave the boys their share of the family land and some money daddy set aside for them. What I hadn't anticipated was her giving y'all the brewery."

"How does Uncle Brandon feel about that?" Nic asked.

He was her grandmother's only son. She couldn't imagine being cut out of the family's business. Especially since, according to her grandmother's journal, he'd help her build it.

"Don't get me to lying, chile," Shelby said as an answer.

Which could mean anything from 'I don't know' to 'I think I know, but won't speculate.' Nicole was anxious to get back to her grandmother's journal. Her phone beeped, and she saw a message from Marcellus asking her to come over when she could. Perfect. If he was already looking into Grandmother's murder, then she was no longer alone in that. For the first time in weeks, since she'd made the decision, she felt lighter.

Chapter Seven

From the sounds below, the club was in full swing. JT finished dressing, sliding up a pair of worn jeans and a black 'Lore' T-shirt. He pulled off his du-rag and slid a hand across his waves. Grabbing his leather saddlebag, he headed downstairs. The back hallway was empty, and his office locked as he'd left it. He walked towards the bar and peeked his head in. His cousin Emily was in place, filling glasses.

"Em, you straight?"

She nodded and passed off the glasses to her customers. "Everyone is behaving. How'd it go?"

"Same ol'," he answered.

She smiled and went back to work.

He unlocked his office and took a deep inhale, filtering through scents. Finding nothing unusual, he settled into his leather chair and emptied his saddlebag on the top of his desk. He counted through the thirty g's he'd made on his run. The ride to Columbus only took him four hours, but the territory they drove through was delicate. He was happy to be back, with no trouble. The west Georgia wolves were wild, and the magic-wielders damn near lawless. It took a lot of finessing. It was why he never passed off the run to anyone. He'd transported some crazy shit to them a time or two: dangerous magical items, some dark, some not. Either way, he didn't want to risk his wolves.

He spun his chair and opened his safe, sliding the stacks in there to join the others. He'd add it to the drop for the club at the bank tomorrow. Another plus side of small-town life. He had cousins every damn where, and his family always looked out for each other. He'd drop the money off to his cousin Julissa, and she'd make sure to spread it out among the pack's many accounts. He was making notes in the ledger when his cousin Dante walked in. Tall and lean like most of his cousins, Dante stalked into his office, the power of his wolf preceding him.

"What it do, cousin?" Dante slapped down a few stacks to JT's desk. "Fifty g's."

JT grunted and made a note. "Anybody short?"

"Nope, it's all there."

"Problems?"

It was the same conversation they had every time they met.

"Nah, Curtis got stopped in Brantley County and searched, but he was carrying 'cooking herbs,' so they let him go."

"Cop touch it at all?"

"Sniffed a couple of bottles, according to Curtis. Brought the dogs out, but let him go after he dialed Bev." Dante answered.

JT nodded. Bev was the lawyer they had on retainer, another cousin. He turned and opened the safe.

"Anything else going on?"

JT sighed, reaching for the stacks. "Need you to ride to Albany for me, or send someone up. Jus said she heard some rumors."

"Wulfen up that way?"

He nodded and closed the safe.

"Reckless fucking kids, man."

JT gave him a crooked smile, "we were reckless kids once upon a time."

"Our OGs ain't play that, though."

"You right." The smile dropped from his face. "Jus said they were just looking for shit to move at this point. Find out what you can."

"What you doing about Ms. Patsy?" Dante asked.

JT shrugged. "I'm working on it. I talked to Cellus and Bev. They gave me the file they got from the police."

"Not for nothing, but I think it's a human. Everything supernatural in this part of the world knows better than to fuck with us." Dante pointed out.

"I thought of that. I put some feelers out, so we'll see."

There was a short knock on his door before Dante could ask another question. Another of his cousins peeked her head through the door. Yara was statuesque, her dark skin gleaming under the lights. A lot of dark skin.

"The fuck is you wearing, Yara?" Dante growled, sitting up in his chair.

JT shook his head. She wore a pair of painted-on jeans and some kind of criss-cross top that bared more skin than it covered. Yara ignored Dante's question, setting down what looked like ten thousand dollars.

JT grabbed it and slid it into his top drawer. "Any issues?"

"Nah, run went smooth," she answered.

"Your mate know you left the house like that?" Dante cut in. "Did you go on your run like that?"

Yara sucked her teeth. "Mind your damn business, and no, I did not."

Dante pulled out his phone and snapped a picture. "Yeah, I'm finna send her a picture of your ass so she can see what you out here looking like."

Yara reached for the phone, and Dante held it out of her reach. She smacked his arm laughing, reaching again.

"Nah, she need to get your wild ass under control."

Yara moved fast, her body a shadowy blur as she snatched the phone. Dante was a hair slower than her.

She flipped through it smugly. "I know you ain't talking, all these hoes you got on your phone."

"Give me my shit," Dante said, snatching the phone back and slipping it into his pocket.

"Anyways," she slid a folded note from her pocket. "Got a couple of orders for you. Bishop gave your info to a witch outside of Macon."

JT slipped the paper with the other orders he needed to handle.

"I'm dancing tonight...with my damn mate," she gave Dante a pointed look. "let me know if you need me."

He nodded. "A'ight then, cuz."

"Bye, jackass," she mushed Dante's face.

"Love you too, baby sister," Dante taunted.

JT shook his head at their antics. "You staying too?"

"Yep, heard Ness was back in town. I'm trying to see something."

"You don't learn, do you?"

Dante shrugged. "It is what it is."

He left JT in his office alone before he could say anything else. Not that he would. Dante and Ness had a complicated history, and it wasn't his business. Nicole, on the other hand. He thought long and hard about making her his business. He pulled her face up from memory. His wolf sat forward, power filling his body.

She had to be close for her wolf to react that way.

He reached out his senses, smiling in satisfaction. Indeed she was.

Chapter Eight

"Lord have mercy," Nicole muttered under her breath.

Ness snickered next to her, popping down the mirror and checking her lipstick. "You so scary."

Nicole eyed the gravel parking lot staring at the many motorcycles scattered across it. There weren't this many when she'd stopped by yesterday. Maybe because it was dark, but everything looked more dangerous. She gave Vanessa a look.

"Maybe we should come back in the afternoon."

Ness snorted, "nonsense, we good here."

She got out of the car, and Nicole had no choice but to follow. They were waved inside by the burly guy at the door. It was certainly louder than it was that afternoon. Rap music blared out of the speakers, and there were people crowded around the two pool tables. It wasn't as bad as she imagined it would be by the motorcycles. Yes, there were some dangerous-looking men in there, some fine as hell ones too. She licked her lips. Ness bopped over to one of the only open tables and sat. She caught the bartender's eyes and waved. He nodded, and Ness settled in her chair. Nicole looked around, and JT wasn't at the bar. She suppressed a disappointed feeling and reminded herself that she had no time for shenanigans.

A young woman came up with a tray under her arm. "What can I get you?"

"We'll have two of the SpringBrooks," Nic ordered.

The girl nodded and walked off to get their order.

"This place has changed a lot. It looks way better than before," Ness said over the music.

"You've been here before?"

Ness nodded, and then her face lit up.

Nicole turned and looked over her shoulder and spotted JT making his way through the crowd. His body seemed to eat up space, his walk more of a prowl. He walked like he was carrying something heavy between his legs. She squirmed in her seat, all manner of fantasies starting. He wore black on black, fitted black jeans, and a sleeveless black shirt. Tattoos covered his dark skin from wrist to shoulder, disappearing underneath his shirt. Ness stood up and walked around the table to meet him. Nicole turned in her seat to observe their interaction.

"If it isn't Jeremiah Taylor," Ness said, holding out her arms.

JT grabbed her up and lifted her, planting a kiss on her cheek. "Look what the cat done dragged in."

Ness threw back her head and laughed as JT set her down on her six-inch heels. Nicole pushed down on her jealousy. Clearly, the two of them knew each other. Ness sat back down, and JT stood next to the table. His dark gaze settled on her, and he licked his full lips, rubbing a hand against his well-groomed beard.

"Y'all know each other?" She asked.

"Me and JT go way back," Ness answered.

He lifted the corner of his mouth in a slight smirk. "Drinks are on me," he told them. "I'll be right back."

She felt naked under his gaze, but not in a way she didn't like, which was kind of a problem. He turned towards the bar, dapping up patrons as he made his way through the crowd. Nic wondered how well her cousin knew JT but would bite her tongue off before asking.

Ness cut into her thoughts. "It's not like you think. His family helped me control this cat we share our skin with. Ugly and all."

"Ain't nothing wrong your cat," JT scolded, coming back with their drinks. He'd intercepted the waitress.

"It's unnatural," Ness told him.

JT laughed. "Who am I to judge a kink?" He leaned down and kissed Ness again.

He raked his gaze across Nicole in an assessing way that felt dangerous, at least to her. He brushed a finger down her cheek. The touch was familiar, and they didn't know each other, so why did he even feel like he could do it? Her heart raced with the contact, her cat attracted to the air of menace that surrounded him. He leaned over, and his cheek touched hers, his breath brushing across her ear.

She shuddered, her stomach clenching with lust.

"Let me know if you need anything, hear," he whispered.

Nic wanted to say something clever in response, but her breath was stuck in her throat. JT winked and left, and Nic whipped her gaze to Ness.

"How well do you know him?"

"I didn't leave Georgia until high school, so me and JT damn near grew up together. He's the new alpha of his family's pack."

Nic swallowed down the unearned jealousy and swung her gaze back to him. "Alpha?"

"It means he's the biggest, baddest shifter in these parts," Ness claimed, chugging her beer. "Oh shit, this is really good!"

She ignored that and got back to what she wanted to know. "So his whole family knows about our...." Nic looks around, "our curse?" She whispered.

Ness leaned in, "everybody in this bar knows," her cousin whispered loudly. "Hell, everyone in this area knows the Fouche women. I don't doubt that they know about the curse."

Nic sat back, stunned. Was that why she got so many stares as she went around town? Ness stood and reached out her hand.

"Come on, let's shake off some of this stress."

Nic grabbed her hand and joined her on the dance floor, such as it was. It was just a small circle in the middle of the tables, but it was filled nonetheless. She had fun with Ness. None of the men in the bar bothered them. She figured it had something to do with the looks JT shot any person that came near them. Either way, she enjoyed it. After a couple of hours, though, she'd had enough. They'd only come in to have a beer so that Ness could taste their grandmother's creation. The dancing was a bonus.

Nicole pulled her cousin from the dance floor. She had a meeting in the morning and didn't want to be out all night. "Time to go."

Ness pouted. "Already?"

"I got somewhere to be in the morning."

"Fine, let me go say bye to JT." Even as Ness said that her eyes were on someone else.

Nicole followed her line of vision to a massive man standing at the pool table eyeing them. The man looked dangerous, his black shirt and leather motorcycle vest emblazoned with the Taylor insignia. Someone else Ness knew? It wasn't her business, so she tore her eyes away from him and followed Ness to the bar.

Ness had found JT and pulled him down into a hug. "We leaving."

"You good to get back?" JT directed the question to them both.

Nicole nodded. "I only had one drink." She licked her lips, her mouth suddenly dry.

He gave her a small smile, "Alright then, Fouche."

"It's Oliver," she said over the music.

The heated stare he gave her was making her reckless. He licked his lips but said nothing to her correction.

The side of his lips quirked into a small smile. "Good night y'all. Let me know when you get home safe, hear Ness."

"Got it," Ness said and pulled Nic with her towards the door.

She gave one final look back to JT and found him staring. She should be glad Ness was with her; otherwise, what reckless thing would she have done?

Chapter Nine

Nic slowed down her car and frowned as her headlights illuminated another vehicle in her grandmother's driveway.

"Who is that?" Ness asked.

"I don't know."

They both got out and approached the house cautiously. She grabbed her mace out of her purse.

"I know that's right," Ness whispered and reached into her own purse.

"Oh, that's a cute taser," Nic paused at the jewel-encrusted device Ness gripped.

"Right?!"

They proceeded up the front porch. Seeing no one waiting, Nic unlocked the door and slowly walked in.

"About doggone time," a voice said from the kitchen.

Ness sucked her teeth. "Audrey?"

The person in question came around the corner from the kitchen, a sandwich in her hand. "Where y'all been?"

"I thought you weren't due for another few days." Nicole dropped her mace back into her purse.

Audrey shrugged, her eyes losing their brightness. "Plans change."

Nicole raked her eyes over her cousin, searching for clues of her. She hadn't talked to Audrey as much as she did Ness. They weren't as close, seeing as Aunt Kit was another person Lauren liked to fight with. Audrey was petite, delicate even, her curves nowhere near as thick as hers and Ness's. Her cousin had dyed her short curly, tapered hair auburn, and the color contrasted with her mahogany skin beautifully.

Ness walked over and hugged her. "You look beautiful! I'm so happy you're here!"

"Yeah, me too," Nic said, walking over and gripping Audrey's shoulder in greeting.

"You guys pick out your rooms?" Audrey asked as she polished off her sandwich.

"Yep," Ness confirmed, kicking off her heels. "I'm headed to bed. Can we catch up in the morning?"

"Sounds good," Audrey answered.

"Need help getting your stuff in?" Nic asked her softly.

Audrey shook her head, the gold hoops shaking with the motion. "I did all that while y'all were out."

Nic nodded. "Okay, well...I guess I'll see you in the morning."

She kicked off the heels she wore and picked them up, walking barefoot up the stairs to the room she'd picked out. She was not as close to Audrey, but her heart felt lighter having her cousin under the same roof. It felt right to have them all here. She smiled, happy she'd decided to come.

The following morning, Nicole found herself navigating the dirt roads to her cousin Marcellus's house. She probably could've walked, but she hadn't been dancing in a long time, and last night had caught up to her. Even in the slides she now wore, her feet were hurting. It had been worth it, though. She parked behind her cousin's truck and got out, smiling at the bicycles scattered across the front yard.

She knocked on his door, and it opened, a petite person peering up at her. She smiled. "Hi, is your dad home?"

The shy child made no moves, instead staring with those unmistakable cat-like eyes. It clicked who she was, and Nic smiled.

She signed. *"I'm your cousin, Nicole. Can I come in?"*

Her eyes widened, a smile breaking out across her face.

"Yes, come in," the little girl signed.

Nicole walked into the house and closed the door. She took a look around, impressed with the warm home her cousin kept.

"Get your shoes on, and let's go. I'm not trying to be late to church," Beverly yelled out. Marcellus's wife rounded the corner and gasped in surprise. "Nicole, hi!"

"Brina let me in," she said aloud as well as signed.

Sabrina passed a chagrined look to her mother.

"Brina should have her stockings and shoes on already," Beverly signed and said aloud, her eyes cutting to her middle child.

"Going now," Brina rolled her eyes and signed. *"Nice to meet you."* The little girl hightailed it from the foyer.

Beverly turned her attention to Nicole, a smile on her beautiful face. "You know how to sign?"

"I learned it for my job, and then when you guys had Brina, I made sure to keep up with it," she said sheepishly.

Beverly touched a hand to her chest. "That's...thank you, Nic. You don't even see her like that, and you still...."

Nic cleared the lump from her throat, "She's growing up so beautiful."

"Right? And has the nerve to look exactly like her grandmother.

Shelby won't let me hear the end of it." Beverly said, stepping into heels. "Let's go, monsters, I ain't got all morning!"

She snickered. "Cellus in the back?"

"His office is down the hall. Will you be by Shelby's for dinner?"

"Yep."

"I'll see you then," Beverly said, rushing off.

Nicole dodged a preteen speeding through the house at his mother's call and walked down the hallway, peering at the pictures on the wall.

She found her cousin behind a classy white desk, two wide monitors spread across it.

"You skipping church, Marcellus," Nicole tsked.

He lifted his head from the monitor and smiled. "You ain't dressed either, Nicole Oliver."

She snorted and walked in. He circled the desk and pulled her into a hug, lifting her off the ground.

Nicole cupped his cheek, "how you doing?"

She saw the strain around his eyes. She knew how close he was to their grandmother.

He sighed and stepped back, wiping his face. "I'm getting through each day."

"So..." she tried to figure out how to bring it up. Failing, she decided to just get to it. "Aunt Shelby said that you've been talking with the police?"

He nodded and went back around his desk. "Yeah." His eyes flashed with anger. "They've been pussyfooting around."

"Have they given you anything?" She sat down in the chair across from his desk.

He shook his head. "Just keep riding the line about it being an intruder."

"And you don't believe that?"

"Absolutely not."

She released the breath she was holding. "Me either."

He looked stunned, and for a moment, relief relaxed his face. "Did you come to do something about it?"

"Hopefully," she said softly.

He dropped his head onto his desk.

She hastily swiped the tear that ran down her cheek. "What do you have so far?"

He sat back and unlocked a drawer, pulling out an envelope. He slid out pictures of what looked like the crime scene.

She scooted to the end of her chair. "How in the hell did you get these?"

"Bev has contacts. You know how small this place is. Everyone knows everyone."

She nodded, set her bag on his desk, and grabbed the pictures. She went through them. She had seen plenty of images of the devastation left behind in natural disasters; still, nothing prepared her for the scenes. She swallowed down a lump as she saw her grandmother's house trashed. The same place she'd left in pristine condition this morning. She hissed when she saw the picture of the pool of blood and the statue.

"They left out the actual pictures. I didn't..." he broke off.

"Of course, no one wants to see that," she murmured. She picked up the picture of the bloody statue. "This was Grandmother's?"

It was a citizen award that she'd likely gotten from the rotary club she frequented. It was glass, and the corner of it was covered in blood.

"They didn't get prints off of it?"

Marcellus sucked his teeth. "A lot of prints. Everyone in this damn family had prints on that thing. We were there when she got it. It was just a week or so before she died."

She sucked in a surprised breath. "Was anything stolen?"

"Not that we can tell," Marcellus said. "The police are trying to say that some druggy went through her medicine cabinet."

She snorted. Her grandmother didn't take modern medicine.

"My reaction as well. Ain't nobody killing our grandmother over herbal supplements."

"Homemade ones at that," Nic murmured. She shuffled the pictures back into the envelope and gave her cousin her attention. "Where do we start, you think?"

Marcellus gave her a chagrined look. "I don't have the foggiest. It took me forever just to get the records. I asked JT if he would ask around."

That shocked her. She brought up the image of him last night at his club. Something about him made her feel reckless. The air of danger that surrounded him warned her that she should be careful, but hormones were winning out. It didn't' help that she heard about him everywhere she went, from her grandmother's journal, to now Cellus mentioning him. He seemed intertwined all through her family. It was probably best that she left him alone.

"He got pull like that?" She asked, thinking of Ness' words from last night.

"He's the Alpha around here. Usually, the Taylors keep a pretty tight lid on crime in the area." He wiped a hand across his face. "He's pretty invested in finding out who came into their territory and did this. That's a good thing for us."

She pulled out the journal. "I was hoping by going through this we can maybe find someone who had a motive. JT's name is in here a lot. Grandmother had dealings with him?"

His hands shook as he pulled her journal close to him. He opened it, and his eyes watered as he ran his hands over her script. He cleared his throat. "They did business together. Grandmother sold herbs and potions and stuff through him."

She frowned. "And you think that could be motive for murder?"

He shrugged. "Any luck finding someone else in here?"

"I just started." She admitted.

He nodded.

"We're really gonna do this?" She asked.

"I'm not letting someone get away with killing our grandmother," he growled.

"Agreed. I'm going to look through the journal, but I was hoping you could ask your brother about stuff at the brewery."

He winced. "Dame doesn't want to get involved."

Nic scoffed. "That's not surprising; he has an infant to worry about."

"Right. I'll ask around, though. Now that you guys have inherited the brewery, you can ask Uncle Brandon questions, too."

"You think her small microbrewery would make enemies? Budweiser got shooters?"

He snorted. "I'm checking everything. Besides, I don't know how much you and Grandmother talked about on the phone, but the microbrewery is no longer small. She and Uncle Brandon built it up, it does good business."

"How big?" She asked, curious.

"Big enough for Damian to make a good living off of it." Was his answer.

Another shock. "Grandmother always downplayed it when we talked. I never knew."

"Speaking of which...when did you learn that you'd inherit everything?"

"Whatever, boy. I found out exactly two weeks ago when the lawyer found me in Texas."

His eyes widened. "Grandmother didn't tell you guys you'd be inheriting?"

"Not me at least, and the way Ness was talking, I don't think she knew either. I hadn't talked to her in the two weeks I'd been working in Texas."

"Wow. She called the three of us over to her house for dinner and went over some stuff. She asked if we wanted it. Julian's in Atlanta, and Dame said he's not cut out for it. He just likes the science of it all. Besides, once we found out that grandfather had left us a trust fund and not you guys, we figured it was only fair."

She nodded. "The first place police look is at the family. Should we be doing the same?"

He looked alarmed. "I honestly don't see how it could be any of us, but you aren't as close as the rest of us, so you're in a place to look at it with fresh eyes."

She winced at that assessment. "Fair enough. We're supposed to see the lawyer Tuesday morning. I'll start asking questions."

"Let me know what you find?"

"Of course."

Nicole's mind was spinning when she left his office an hour or so later. She needed to go through the paperwork the lawyer had sent her because she, Vanessa, and Audrey had inherited a sizeable estate from what Marcellus told her. Had her mother known? Surely Lauren would've said something if she realized Grandmother had built her brewery up as big as Cellus said. What else had she missed being gone for so long?

Chapter Ten

Ness and Audrey were in the kitchen making breakfast when she got back to their grandmother's house. She smiled, distracted, her mind still on her meeting with Marcellus.

"Where did you go?" Audrey asked.

"To see Cellus," she answered, sitting at the table.

"Dang, without us," Ness fussed.

She smiled, "we had some stuff to talk about."

"How is he?" Audrey asked, sitting down next to her with a plate.

"You can see his grief." Nic shook her head.

"He was close to Grandmother, has been since forever," Ness commented.

She nodded.

"What do you want to do today?" Audrey asked.

"I want to go through some of Grandmother's things," Nic answered.

"Okay. Have breakfast with us," Ness coaxed.

She nodded and washed her hands, and fixed her plate.

"Where did you two go last night?" Audrey asked as she sat.

"To Lore," Ness answered.

Audrey wrinkled her nose. "The motorcycle club, it's still standing?"

"JT done fixed it up. It looks good." Ness said.

"What in the world do you know about Lore?" Nicole looked between her two cousins. She knew they stayed in Georgia after she and her mother left, but she hadn't realized how much longer.

"It was one of mama's drinking spots. I've pulled her out of there more times than I can count." Audrey shrugged.

"So you know they're werewolves?" Was the whole town full of shifters? It would make sense in a way, but even in her work, she'd never encountered an entire town of shifters.

Ness rolled her eyes, "Shifters, girl."

"Same difference."

"If you say so," Ness said.

Audrey nodded. "I forgot how sheltered Aunt Lauren had you. You couldn't go nowhere farther than these yards,"

Nic sucked her teeth, unable to dispute that.

"Back to the subject at hand, why were y'all hanging out at a motorcycle club? Ain't nothing but drug dealers and bikers there."

Ness snorted. "Judgey."

"I'm not judging, just saying." Audrey disputed.

"The Taylors are not drug dealers," Ness argued.

Nicole thought that was probably a stretch. She didn't imagine the Taylors led a motorcycle club just to ride bikes. If they weren't dealing drugs, they were likely dealing in something else. She didn't say anything, though.

"That ain't what mama said."

"Auntie Kit don't know everything, Audrey." Ness snapped.

Her cousin just shrugged. She smiled at their bickering.

"I saw the way you were looking at JT. You think he dealing drugs too?" Ness directed her attention to her.

Nic scooped up her food and didn't answer.

"So you would sleep with him, thinking he was a drug dealer?"

Nic choked.

"Wait, you're sleeping with JT?" Audrey asked.

"Not yet, but her little fast behind was undressing him with her eyes," Ness waggled her eyebrows.

She drank her juice to stop coughing. "Stay out of my business."

"See," Ness said.

"He was cute when we were little. What he look like now?" Audrey asked, leaning forward.

"Fine as hell," Ness answered.

Nic gave her a sharp look. Ness laughed.

"See that look, she wanna ride the dick," Ness said triumphantly.

"Oh my God, this is a lot over breakfast," Nic protested.

Audrey and Ness laughed even harder.

JT closed his ledger and stood and stretched. He was restless. A new feeling for him. He liked his life and enjoyed the predictable nature of it. Outside of his illegal runs, he didn't run into much in their small town. His mind drifted to Nicole. She was one of the reasons his wolf was so restless. The woman had gotten under his skin. Just her mere presence made him nervous. He needed to find something to do. Leaving his office, he walked into the bar, expecting to find it empty. It was Sunday, after all. Instead, he found the object of his thoughts sitting at the bar alone, a glass of water slowly gathering condensation on his bar top. He looked around for any of his employees but saw no sign of them.

He leaned his shoulder onto the doorway and crossed his arms over his chest, studying her. She was a beautiful thing, and somehow, instead of off-putting, he found all that broodiness to be attractive. The way her lips would pout, the darkness swirling around her eyes, all of it. JT sighed and gave in to the instinct. He moved to pretty

Nicole Oliver. She looked up at him, and her dark eyes, tilted up at the corners, were mesmerizing.

She pierced him with those exotic eyes. "A guy named Dante let me in, said he'd be right back."

Her husky voice moved through him, the growly tone rubbing over his skin. It was the only excuse he had for his next question for her.

"I was headed out for a ride on my bike. Wanna come?" He slid a coaster underneath her glass.

Her eyes widened, and she licked her lips. He leaned forward on the bar, not to take the kiss he desperately wanted, just to get a little closer to her scent.

"On your motorcycle?"

He nodded. "You wanna ride?"

Her eyes went slumberous, the double entendre hitting its mark.

"I've never been on a motorcycle."

"Come on. It'll clear some of those cobwebs out of your brain."

She brushed a hand down her hair. "I could use the air."

He smiled, and her heartbeat kicked up a notch. He nodded his head towards the door, and she slid out of the stool. He waited until she walked around and slid under the opening at the bar. He walked her through the back hallway and out the side door where he kept his bike. Her eyes went wide again.

"Now, that's a bike."

"Ain't she pretty," he said with a laugh.

She nodded and slid her hands down the side of the gas tank and over the leather seat. Would've thought it was his body she touched with the way his dick jumped. He sighed. This definitely wasn't a good idea. He was happy he'd pulled out the larger of his Indian Chiefs. He had two, but this one was a two-seater. The bike was low the ground, matte black, and customized to carry a larger payload if needed. He handed her the helmet he kept stored and helped put it on her head. She smiled at him, and his heart did a slow tumble. Another sigh, this one internal. He was fucked. His wolf, on the other hand, was near smug in the fact that they'd cheered her up. He got on the back.

"Up you go, Fouche."

She straddled his bike, her thighs buffering his hips. She gripped his shoulders, and he shuddered as need slammed into him. It would be a long ride.

"Hold on tight, hear?"

She slid closer, her hands going around his waist. He prayed her hands stayed high because lord have mercy, just a little lower and she'd meet steel. He lifted the kickstand and kicked down to start the motor. She squealed when the powerful engine started, the vibrations rumbling the seat. She squirmed behind him, and JT figured he was due sainthood if he made it through this ride.

"Ready?"

She nodded on his back, and he took off. He expected her to scream. She didn't, just gripped him tighter as he took off towards the highway.

He headed towards 95, intending to circle a couple of exits and let her feel the power of his machine. They went two exits, and he turned off, taking the backroads back to his family's territory. He slowed down as they came to the river, pulling up to the small fishing dock. He helped her down, and they walked over to the dock. He plopped on the edge and pulled her down next to him. She closed her eyes and inhaled in the air.

"The coastline is disappearing, but I love this area," he commented.

"I don't know what it is about this place," she murmured.

They sat in silence for a few minutes.

"What's on your mind?"

"Grandmother. I've been trying to figure out who to ask to figure out what she was up to the last weeks of her life." She crossed her legs.

His eyebrows winged high. "Have you tried the police?"

"Fuck the police," she muttered.

He chuckled. A woman after his own mind. "Well, let me see what I remember."

He thought back to what Ms. Patsy had been doing, any items she'd asked him to run. She had been gathering some pretty powerful things lately, but he hadn't known what for.

"Ms. Patsy had me currying some of the magical ingredients she made to a few contacts she has in North Georgia." He said finally.

She turned to him. "That's what you courier? Magical items?"

He didn't deny or affirm. "Why?"

She shrugged, "me and Audrey assumed it was drugs."

He snorted. "Nothing like that."

"Audrey will feel better."

"Y'all been talking about me?"

She leaned her head on her knees. "I find you very attractive, Jeremiah Taylor, but I don't sleep with drug dealers, too much family history around drugs."

His heart rate picked up. "Oh, we'll be sleeping together?"

She stared at him with those dark, broody eyes. "I'm still thinking about it."

"You're very upfront," He commented idly.

"I don't know any other way to be. If I'm not explicit and upfront, both my parents would run right over me."

He nodded, adding that little piece to the picture he was building of her. The corner of his mouth tilted up. His wolf was delighted. He lifted her chin with his finger.

"Seems I should have a say in that. Let me see if I'd be interested."

He leaned closer, slowly, giving her a chance to back away. When she didn't, he sealed their lips together. She opened her mouth, and he delved his tongue inside, tasting her, his body tightening in anticipation. Their kiss was slow, exploratory, the kind of kiss two potential lovers would share. He leaned further into the kiss, overwhelmed with how amazing her lips felt. Every sweep of her tongue sent fire coursing through him. From the heat burning through him, setting his face aflame, he was absolutely interested. He knew they could be good together. His wolf brushed against his skin, his power surging through his body. There was no question of his wolf's interest. Not like the animal hadn't let him know from the moment she walked into his bar.

She pulled back slowly, reluctantly. "Since we're contemplating sleeping together, you should know my last name is not Fouche."

He smiled. "So you've told me."

She shook her head. "But you're gonna call me that anyways."

He leaned over and kissed her again, committing her taste to his memory. He would call her whatever she wanted, just to be able to touch her.

"I know both of your cousins, but I don't remember you." He wanted to add more to that picture.

"We left when I was six. Barely in the first grade. Mom let me come back a few summers, at least until I was like eleven."

"What happened then?"

"My parents split."

He didn't know what that felt like. Wolf shifters mated for life, and his parents were still together, happily.

"And you came back all these years because of your grandmother?" He prompted.

"She left us an inheritance. But mostly, I don't like the way she died. I won't be able to rest until I find out what happened. I've failed my grandmother in so many other ways. I don't want to fail her in this."

"So you came to my bar to brood?" He teased.

"It's a good broody place."

He snorted, liking her sense of humor. "Have you talked to your cousin Marcellus?"

She nodded. "He said you were going to ask around?"

"It don't look right, people dying in my territory with me knowing about it. People start to get ideas."

"You only like murders that you know about?" She cut him a look.

"It's a hard world out here, Fouche," And the world he inhabited wasn't built for the squeamish.

She sighed. "I've realized that finding my grandmother's killer without local help would be all but impossible."

He smirked. "Are you asking me for help?"

She worried her bottom lip with her teeth a moment before she spoke. "Your name keeps coming up in my family. I figure the universe is trying to tell me something."

He considered her, his gaze raking her beautiful face. She was looking off into the marsh, a weary set to her shoulders. She was trying hard to hide it, but he could see the grief all over her. His wolf whined, urging him to reach for her and offer comfort. That was a dangerous idea, so he proposed the safer option...

"I'll help where I can."

She turned to him. "Really? Thank you, I appreciate it."

He could tell her that he'd planned to look into it anyway, but he liked the thought her of gratitude. Plus, as a bonus, he would get to spend time with her. His wolf liked that idea a lot.

Chapter Eleven

er first week in her grandmother's house had passed, and she'd found nothing in the way or clues or motive. Nicole was getting frustrated with the lack of progress. She was running out of ideas, and it didn't help that she couldn't get a particular wolf out of her head. She dropped the towel and slipped on a nightgown.

Aside from the dead-ends, she loved being back at her grandmother's house. The longer she stayed, the more at home she felt. While it wasn't a given that she would stay, every day, that possibility of her living here started to feel real. So far, she and her cousins were getting along, and they would make good roommates. She knew the most challenging part would probably be telling her mother that she'd decided to stay. Lauren would flip her shit and lay the thickest of thick guilt trips on her. She sighed and settled into bed.

Her phone rang no sooner than she'd snuggled under the sheets. She frowned at the private number. Curiosity propelled her to pick up.

"Hello?"

"Fouche."

JT's deep voice moved through her body, and goosebumps traveled down her skin. It should be a crime to sound that good. She swallowed and pretended nonchalance.

She sucked her teeth, "It's Oliver."

"mmhmm," he hummed.

"How did you get my number?"

"Town ain't but so big, Fouche."

She rolled her eyes, knowing he was doing it on purpose at this point. "Why did you call?"

"Just wanted to see what you were doing."

She looked over at the bedside clock. "At 11 pm?" she said dryly.

He chuckled, not in the least bit offended. "Now see, you ain't even let me finish my sentence. What are you doing tomorrow?"

A whole lot of nothing. But of course, she didn't tell him that.

"Why?" She asked brusquely, which seemed to amuse him all the more.

"I'm coming by to pick you up."

"Me?" She sat up in shock, "why?"

"I want to take you somewhere."

"Like where?"

"I want to show you a little piece of your grandmother. You seemed interested in what she'd been up to..." he trailed off, and she snapped right at the bait.

"Yes," she said hastily.

He chuckled, "It'll be early."

"That's fine. I wake up at the crack of dawn anyway."

"So, how are you liking life in the country so far?" He asked.

She sighed. "I was just thinking about that. I like it."

"How long y'all staying?"

"That's the six million dollar question," she whispered.

He grunted.

"Where are you taking me tomorrow?"

"It's a surprise."

"I don't like surprises," she grumbled.

He laughed. "Now, how did I know you would say that?"

She couldn't help the smile that lifted her lips. "So anyway," she changed the subject. She froze as something tapped against the window. "Oh shit," she whispered.

The door to her room burst open, and Ness flew in with a bat over her shoulders. "Did you hear that?" Ness asked.

Nicole pushed the covers from her legs and stood. "I did," she whispered.

"It's the same as last night," Ness said.

Audrey rushed in next. "Someone is outside of my window," she hissed.

"What's happening?" JT demanded on the phone.

"Someone is trying to get into the house," she whispered into the phone, reaching the drawer of her bedside table and pulling out a stun gun.

Another tap sounded, and Audrey lifted the gun in her hand.

Ness's eyes widened. "You have a gun in here."

"Girl, I don't go anywhere without my gun." Audrey snapped.

"I'm coming over," JT barked into the phone.

Before she could tell him no, he hung up. Nicole tossed her phone down on the bed and followed her cousins from the room.

"Should we go outside?" Audrey whispered.

"Hell no, but if they make the mistake of coming in, their ass is grass," Nicole said.

"Agreed," Ness said, holding her bat on her shoulder, ready to swing.

They slowly went through all the rooms, and when nothing else sounded, they headed down to the living room. From there, they could hear the loud rumbly sound of a motorcycle engine. They waited in tense silence as it shut off. There was a knock on the door moments later. Even knowing who it was, they all jumped in alarm, Audrey squealing. Nic rolled her eyes at their foolishness and headed for the front door. She looked through the glass just to be safe and exhaled as she recognized the giant form of JT. She opened the door, and he slipped inside. He wore a pair of low-slung jogging pants and a black t-shirt.

"Y'all alright?"

They all nodded.

"I did a lap around the house and didn't find anything, but there are a couple of different scents at the windows."

"Oh shit," Ness whispered. "Who is doing this?"

JT eyed them all. "Been happening a lot?"

"Since I got here, at least. Nic?" Ness answered.

She cleared her throat. "Yeah, I've been hearing things since I arrived. Nothing as loud as tonight, though. Whatever it was, it actually shook my window." She looked to Audrey.

"Same," her cousin said shakily.

He studied them and didn't say anything. "Am I the only one who knows you're asking around about your grandmother?"

Nic shifted a nervous glance to her cousins. They gave her incredulous looks.

"You're looking into the murder?" Ness asked carefully.

She shrugged, "Cellus and me. JT is helping."

Audrey gave out a huff of relieved breath, "oh, thank God. I thought I would have to do it by myself."

"You've also been looking?" Ness asked.

Audrey nodded.

JT cursed. "So it could be someone trying to scare y'all away. Do you want me to post up here?"

That was incredibly sweet of him, and Nic was touched. But, if Lauren had taught Nicole anything, it was that depending on a man was a nonstarter. It was good advice, seeing how no Fouche woman had escaped the curse.

"We'll be fine," she answered.

He eyed her, and then his gaze flickered down to her stun gun at her side. He gave her a devastating smile that warmed her lady parts.

"I see. I'm not too far from here, so just call me if you need something, hear?"

She nodded and walked him to the front door. She turned around to find her cousins staring at her.

"Girl, you couldn't let that man sleep on this couch so we could get some sleep tonight?" Ness snapped.

"What? We handled it all by ourselves. We didn't need him," she reminded them, waving to their variety of weapons.

"Speak for yourself," Audrey said, shuddering.

"Never mind that, let's get to this business of y'all looking into Grandmother's murder. Why didn't anyone say anything?" Ness asked.

Nic shrugged, "I didn't know if anything would come of it."

All at once, the adrenaline keeping her upright for the past half hour left her body, and Nic shivered. Shit, she should've let JT stay over. There was no way she was sleeping tonight.

"We can all pile into the living room like we used to," Nic suggested. She knew she'd never get any asleep alone in her room.

Relief suffused both Audrey and Ness's faces. They all went upstairs and grabbed blankets and pillows to have a sleepover. Spread out along the two sofas and an air mattress Audrey had found, the three settled in well after one in the morning.

Audrey broke the silence. "Do you guys ever think about the fact that Grandmother was murdered in this house, and we're just living here as if nothing happened?"

"Thanks for that Audrey, I was just about to sleep well," Nic said sarcastically.

Ness snorted.

"No, but for real, you guys."

"Ness, you could always join the rest of us and help solve this case," Nicole circled back to their earlier conversation.

"Chile," Ness said. "You for real?"

"Hell yeah, it don't sit right with me," Audrey chimed in.

"What crime-solving ability do either of you have?" Ness asked, exasperated.

"Same as the police if you ask me," Nic said.

"Except the police have guns," Ness argued.

"Shit, I gotta gun," Audrey pointed out.

Ness sat up. "Let's talk about that. You brought a gun to Grandmother's house?"

"Girl, I don't carry my black ass nowhere in Georgia without packing," Audrey said.

Nic snickered. "And you talking about us hanging out at a motorcycle clubhouse."

"My mama just got saved. She taught me well before that happened."

Nicole laughed aloud, and Ness rolled her eyes and flopped back down. "Y'all done lost your minds."

"You might as well quit fussing; you know you're gonna help," Nic told her.

"Fine, but if it gets too much, I'm out." Ness protested.

"Whatever, heifer. Where do we look first?" Audrey asked.

"Me and Cellus were trying to figure that out. We didn't get anything from the lawyer. Maybe we should look around the brewery. We can ask around and see if Grandmother had any enemies." Nic said.

Ness scoffed, "what kind of enemies could an eighty-year-old make?"

"Girl, you don't know what Grandmother was doing. You see Aunt Shelby out in these streets, maybe Grandmother was too." Nic said flippantly.

They busted out laughing.

"We should also search the house and see if there is anything," Ness added.

"I read some of her journal entries. We could also see if she left any other records," Nic said.

"I've been going through her workshop. I can deep dive in there." Audrey chimed in.

"Good idea. I'm going out with JT tomorrow morning."

Ness sat back up. "Oh, do tell."

"It's nothing. He's just going to show me around."

"Mmhmm, show you around his dick, you mean," Ness said.

Nicole laughed. "I said what I meant."

"Did you even find out if he was dealing drugs?" Audrey asked.

"He doesn't," Nic assured them.

"Guns, human trafficking, what does he do?"

"Lord have mercy, you ain't even start at baker, lawyer, just straight to crime," Ness said exasperated.

"He says he couriers stuff."

"What kind of stuff," Ness asked.

"People," Audrey said under her breath.

Ness threw a pillow at her. "Shut up."

Nicole snorted. "He said he moves magical items?" She held her breath to see what they would say.

"Really?" Audrey perked up.

What the hell? "Why are neither of you surprised?"

"Because, unlike you, our mothers were out here. We done seen some shit." Ness settled back into her sleep position.

"I'm sorry, guys." Nicole's heart ached for them.

All three sisters had chosen different paths to drown out their curses. Her cousins got the more complicated course. She didn't mind having a hundred stepfathers if it meant she didn't have to drag her mother out of bars or from corners and alleys. An awkward silence descended.

"Anywho," Ness said. "What do you think the noise was?"

"Y'all must not want to sleep tonight, like at all," Nicole complained.

"Not you finna chase down a murderer but scared of a random noise," Audrey mocked.

"We're not talking about this anymore," Nicole announced and turned over on the love seat, punching her pillows. She would get some sleep tonight, damn it.

Chapter Twelve

Despite last night's adventures, JT knocked on Ms. Patsy's door a little after six in the morning. The sun was slowly making its way over the trees, so it was dark enough for the air to be still a little cool. A groggy Vanessa opened the door, squinting at him.

"Jeremiah Taylor, I know Mama Valerie taught you better than to come over to people's house this time of the morning."

He kissed her forehead and pushed her inside the house. He found the living room a mess of pallets and sleeping women.

Nic scrambled from her bed on the sofa. "Shit, JT, I'm sorry, I overslept."

He smiled. She was beautiful even first thing in the morning. "It's no problem."

"Ness, can you make some coffee while I get dressed?" Nicole gathered her blankets.

"Mmhmm," Ness said with a sly smile.

"Wear long pants and a long-sleeved shirt," JT yelled up as she ascended the stair.

She nodded and went to do that. JT followed Ness into the

kitchen and did a quick lap around the island. His eyes roamed over all the changes Ms. Patsy had made.

"Kitchen looks great," he commented.

"Your mom said that Dante and them did it," Ness commented.

"Yeah, I just hadn't gotten to see it finished." He leaned against the arch that led into the living room.

"Good for Dante." She murmured.

He narrowed his eyes at her careful wording. She turned and faced him as the coffee brewed.

"So, Nicole..."

"Ain't your business, Ness," he warned her.

She crossed her arms over her chest. "My cousin, my business."

He smirked. "You just being nosy; no need to dress it up."

She snickered. "You trying to say I can't look out for my cousin?"

"You know me well enough to know I wouldn't do anything to hurt your cousin, so we can dispense with the third degree...nosy."

"Where ya'll going?"

"I'm taking her out to the marsh. She asked me what your grand-mother was doing the last few weeks before she died."

"Does it have anything to do with your...line of work?"

He debated answering. He didn't make it a habit of telling his business to everyone. "I moved some stuff for Ms. Patsy, procured some others."

"Was it for something she was working on?"

"You know how your grandmother was. Her business was her own."

Ness nodded and sighed, "Which will probably make this so hard. I don't know what the others are thinking.

"Far as I know, Ms. Patsy had a loyal clientele. Can't see any of them doing this," he offered.

"But the people you work with are dangerous?"

He stared but didn't answer.

"Any ideas?"

He shrugged. "The stuff I move is specialized. The only people who can move it or grow it are in the trade. You don't kill your supplier unless you find another. Since I haven't had a change in clientèle and asks, I'm almost certain that Ms. Patsy wasn't killed behind it. But, I could be wrong, and I'm not going to tell you how to investigate. I'm asking around in our circles, but I told Cellus to follow the money. "

"Grandmother's money?" She frowned and lifted her cup, her gaze introspective.

Nic came up behind him, and he turned, his mouth drying as he saw her in the tight jeans. Lord have mercy, those jeans had to be made specifically for her ass. He wanted to tell her to go back upstairs and put on something frumpier, but his mouth dried up, and it was all he could do to keep from going down to his knees and begging her for a taste. He cleared his throat. She was carrying a pair of water goulashes. Damn, a woman prepared for anything. That made her that much more interesting to him. He didn't know why he was doing this. He should be running for the farthest hill away from the Fouche women, but something about her called to him.

"I don't want to intrude on y'alls thing, but next time I want to go with y'all," Ness interjected.

"Fine by me," he said, absently, happy she wouldn't intrude. "Let's go, Fouche."

Nicole followed him out of the front door and onto the porch.

"Sit," he ordered Nicole.

She raised an eyebrow but sat on her grandmother's top step. He reached down and helped her put the boots on each foot, caressing her leg. Her breath caught, and the moment thickened between them. He wanted to feel her skin. Badly enough that his hands started to shake. He huffed out a breath and stood. Lord, there just might be something to the rumors. There was something about a Fouche woman.

"Alright. Put some of this on." He tossed her a deep woods bug spray. No way could he trust himself to touch her again. "Make sure you spray the back of your neck," he murmured huskily.

She nodded and did as he asked. "Can I bring my camera?"

He narrowed his eyes on her, "as long as you don't shoot anything I ask you not to."

"Deal," she said and rushed back inside.

She came out with the small bag a few minutes later, and he grabbed her hand to help her down. She looked at his motorcycle with excitement.

"We're riding again?"

He shook his head. "Nah, walking." He lifted the supplies he'd left on the porch, and her eyes widened.

"You about to kill me?"

He snickered. "Ain't nobody finna kill you, woman, come on here."

"What's the scythe for?"

"For cutting," he answered vaguely. He swallowed down his laugh as she looked at him skeptically.

"Lord have mercy," she muttered but followed.

She walked next to him silently through the woods, occasionally snapping pics. Once they came to the marsh, she paused.

"It's snakes in here, ain't it."

"Probably," he said, tugging her hand to keep moving.

"Probably?" She tugged her hand out of his. "I'm not walking through no marsh."

"You're safe with me, Fouche. Don't tell me you scared of a little water?"

"Of swamp water, hell yeah."

He laughed, "Come on. We'll be safe, I promise." He moved through the marsh, and she gingerly stepped behind him, her heart racing. "Nicole, I can hear your heartbeat over all these crickets. If I can, predators can."

"Predators. Nah, you gotta take me back."

He chuckled and pulled her into his side. "Deep breaths, Fouche," he ordered, holding her chin in his hand.

He looked into her eyes and fell into the dark orbs. Her magic rose, her eyes changing and snaring him further. Her heavily lashed eyes were sinful, made for late nights in the dark. He could almost see himself leaning over her, his gold chain swinging, the gleam of her teeth as she smiled in satisfaction. She gripped his wrist as images of their sweaty bodies gliding along each other played out in filthy detail through his mind. Her body went pliable, and her breathing slowed to an agonizing exhale. Goosebumps pricked against his skin as their whispered moans sounded around them. Was that real or a part of the vision? He was locked into her gaze, the cat close to the surface and trying to take over. His wolf's power brushed through him, and in turn her. It was as if her cat took a breath, recognizing the strength of his wolf. It backed off, and her power cooled, releasing him from the spell she'd woven around them both.

Shit.

If that was just a hint of the Fouche power...

Nicole took a heaving breath and moved back. He did the same because the vision felt so real. Water splashed against his leg, the cold snapping him out of it. What kind of power did she have? It was wild, untamed, and heady. Dangerous for sure. Ms. Patsy had powers he nor his wolf could quite get a handle on. It would seem her grand-daughter was the same. In the business he was in, he'd seen some magic that surprised him, but none that had touched him like hers. He wondered if she had control over it. From the feel of it, she didn't. It was something he needed to consider.

She shook her head and took another step back, eyeing him, looking for what? A reaction of some sort? She held herself still, her muscles tensed as she waited to see what he would say. He wanted to ask what had happened, but magic users tended to be a secretive bunch; she probably wouldn't answer.

"Interesting," was all he said, and then he grabbed her arm, right above the wrist, careful to avoid touching her skin.

Just in case.

No telling what would happen if he had to go through that erotic vision again. Not that his wolf would object to him stripping her in the middle of this marsh and making those visions come true. The man would rather do that someplace more comfortable. They pushed ahead through the marsh, no other complaints coming from her. She was too shaken to do more than follow him docilely. Soon, though, the swamp sounds filtered through, and she watched as animals moved from their path. She raised her camera again and continued to snap more pictures. It was slightly reassuring.

Every so often, JT would release her hand to cut down a plant from his list. He'd carefully wrap it in the coarse cloth he used for such ingredients and place it in the bottom of the sack he carried. She left him to his work, taking pictures of the wildlife. Every once in a while, he'd shake his head, and she'd lower her camera.

They finally moved out of the marsh onto solid land, and he heard the catch in her breath as they arrived at a spot only he, Dante, and their grandmother knew about. The trees in the area were dense, and light barely reached the ground. Well, sunlight at least. There was light, and most of it came from the flowers that grew there.

"Wow," she whispered. "What is this place?"

"A place only two other people know about."

That was her warning. She nodded, and he relaxed, trusting her, which was...

Yeah, that was new. He'd examine it later.

"Don't touch anything here, 'kay." He warned her.

"Poisonous?" She turned in a circle to take it all in.

"Some. I don't exactly know about all of them. Your grandmother planted half of these."

She looked up at him in surprise. "For what?"

"For whatever Ms. Patsy had going on at the house," he murmured, bending down to gather the plants on his order list.

He went through, checking his list and cutting down the plants needed, leaving the others. Like he'd told Nicole, he didn't know what a lot of them were. Ms. Patsy gave him names for the ones he could sell, but the others were between her and whatever magic she did.

He pointed to a section. "If you want to get pictures of those to look them up, be my guest, so long as you don't let it go past yourself and your cousins. Also, don't touch them with your hands."

He was curious as to what they were personally. Ms. Patsy had warned him not to touch a lot of the stuff back this way. She nodded hastily and did as he asked. He finished his list and watched her as she moved around, taking pictures. He squinted as a few of the plants swayed towards her. Despite his warning, she reached out her hand to touch some of them. The stalks of the ones she caressed grew taller, flowers fuller, the light glowing just a bit more as she moved through them.

Was she aware it was happening?

He got a good look at her face, and her eyes had changed, reflecting gold against the light of the plants. Her cat had taken over again. Feral...that was one word that came to mind when her power brushed through the clearing, calling to the plants that surrounded them. It was astonishing to witness.

"Fouche," he said softly.

She paused her hand over one of the glowing plants and turned to him. Her eyes were darker, her face flush with power. She blinked and seemed to snap out of whatever trance she was in, that power folding back into her body.

"Does that happen often?" He asked in the stillness.

She cleared her throat and nodded. "Sometimes. These plants are...heady. I wasn't expecting it to happen."

He stared, and she lowered her head. He walked to her and lifted her chin, dropping a small kiss against her lips. "That was amazing."

She gripped his wrist. "I don't show that side of myself."

He didn't blame her and felt honored that she'd shown it to him. "I'm finished here. Ready to get out of these mosquitos?"

"Oh God, yes," she breathed out, stepping from him.

He chuckled. "Let's go then, Fouche."

He didn't lead them through the marsh this time, instead,

trekking around it. She sighed in relief when their feet hit the concrete of the road. JT snickered next to her.

"You did good, Fouche."

She rolled her eyes but smiled at the compliment. "Those plants a part of what you and your biker gang move up the interstate?"

He put a hand to his chest. "Dang, we gotta be a gang?"

She snorted. "What other kind of stuff do you...transport?"

He smiled at her careful wording. "All manner of things, Fouche."

"Okay, keep your secrets then."

He chuckled and wrapped an arm around her shoulder as they made the trek back to her grandmother's house. He'd enjoyed his time with her. Had he ever been as relaxed as he was now around a woman, not family? He wanted to spend more time with her. What had started as simple lust was beginning to morph in front of his eyes. JT reminded himself that he was only helping her solve her grandmother's murder and possibly—most definitely if he had his way—fucking her.

That was it.

Getting caught up with Nicole Oliver was not part of the plan.

Chapter Thirteen

"**O**kay, so what do we say when we go in?" Audrey turned from the front seat and stared back at Nic.

Nic sighed and unbuckled her seatbelt. She'd hoped to spend the day going over her morning with JT, but Audrey had had other ideas. So, here they were in the parking lot of the small building that housed her grandmother's microbrewery. The parking lot was near empty, which...she didn't even know what she was expecting. It was Saturday. Did they work on Saturday? Everything she thought she'd known about her grandmother's business was wrong, so she was going into the whole thing blind. According to Cellus, his brother Damian would be there, as well as their Uncle Brandon. The two people she wanted to talk to anyway, so...

Audrey was staring, waiting on one of them to answer her question. Nicole shrugged because honestly, she was winging this finding the murderer shit. Why Nic thought her ability to listen to crime podcasts ad nauseam would lend itself to solving her grandmother's murder, she didn't know. Not that Nicole would tell her parents, but she was slightly in over her head. She gnawed her bottom lip with her teeth and looked over to Ness in the driver's seat.

"Any ideas?"

It was Ness's turn to shrug. "Shit if I know, this was y'alls idea, remember?"

"Okay, well, I'm going to ask for a tour to start. Very non-threatening," Audrey said finally.

"Good, that's good. I need to find a way to work up to seeing the accounting stuff," Nic said softly.

She looked down at the paperwork the lawyer had given them. The folder in her hand had copies of the tax returns for the microbrewery and some kind of internal audit their grandmother had prepared. She was used to seeing budgets in her day job, but it didn't mean she knew anything about the figures the auditor had given to her grandmother—especially the size of these numbers. Marcellus had been right. Their grandmother's company had been doing brisk business. It was imposing, and she was awed by what Patsy had been able to accomplish.

But, all that aside, the math between the two reports wasn't mathing, and she needed to find a way to ask her Uncle about it that didn't seem accusatory. It hadn't raised any alarms with the lawyer, but the three cousins collectively seemed to think something was off.

Technically, neither of them understood the numbers, so they were grasping at straws.

Still, they had to start somewhere. Ness said that JT had told her to follow the money...so here they were.

"He has to give us access, right? That's part of our inheritance," Ness said.

Nic nodded, not entirely sure that would matter. She'd hadn't talked to her Uncle over the years, outside of greetings and the occasional questions about her schooling, so she couldn't say what he'd do or how he would react to them demanding answers.

"Let's go. Tour first, and then we ease into murder accusations," Nic took a deep breath.

Ness snickered and shut off the car. "Uncle Brandon ain't kill nobody."

"You don't know," Audrey shot back.

"Well, I don't believe it," Ness said stubbornly.

She was inclined to agree with Ness. Their Uncle had always been quiet, slow to anger, even when they'd deserved it as kids. She couldn't imagine him flying into a rage to kill his mother. She climbed out of the car and closed the door, squinting at the squat brick building. The front was mostly glass, giving an incredible look into the brewery's inner workings. There was a small bar with metallic tubs behind it. According to Patsy's journal, Uncle Brandon had set up an area for taste tests. The place was currently empty, though she could see someone behind the bar working.

"Is that Aunt Becca?" Ness asked.

Nic nodded and walked towards the building. Their Aunt spied them coming and opened the door. Rebecca was a beautiful woman. She had what her uncle called a coke bottle figure, and she wrapped it in expensive clothes made expressly for her shapely body. There was no hint of gray in her carefully dyed hair. Becca had pulled the auburn strands up into a top knot that showed off her carefully done makeup. She smiled at them as they gathered in the dimly lit room. It smelled of beer and some kind of smoky scent. Nic liked it.

"Girls! I'm so happy you finally came to see us," Becca said cheerfully.

They hugged and walked a circle in the room.

"My God, Aunt Becca, you stay on their necks out here!" Audrey smiled and spun their petite aunt around.

Becca smiled and swatted at Audrey, pleased with the compliment. "Cut it out."

"This looks amazing, Aunt Becca," Ness commented as she looked around.

"Thank you! Brandon did such a great job in here. Did you come by to see him?" Becca asked.

It was posed as an innocent question, but Nic could feel the undercurrents. Her aunt was nervous, and if the hard look in her eyes was anything to go by, a little resentful. It was only there for a nanosecond, but Nic had clocked it and made note.

"We'd love to see Uncle Brandon and Damian and get a tour of a place." Nic put on her work face.

The casual cheerfulness was not innate, but she'd perfected it over the years. People met her when they were going through their worse, and it was her job to reassure them that she'd be able to help them recover, at least their material things. She wiped her mind clear and walked to the bar.

"I'm hoping Damian will give us a taste test. Cellus said he was gifted with hops," Ness infused a brightness into her voice that seemed to relax Aunt Becca.

"That sounds great. Come, let me show you around, and then I'll take you back to Brandon." Aunt Becca weaved her arm through Audrey's and pulled them towards the back.

Becca took them through the whole operation, from start to finish explaining the process. Most of the details went in one ear and out the other as she droned on. Even as Nic smothered her yawn an hour later, she had to admit that it was all very impressive. They finally arrived at her cousin Damian's lab. He jumped up from behind his lab table and rushed to give them hugs. Damian and his brothers all got their height from their father's side of the family, so at six feet tall, he towered over his cousins. He was dressed casually in jeans and a golf shirt with the company logo. His handsome face was slim, a mustache the only facial hair he had. His large dark eyes framed by heavy dark eyebrows showed his lack of sleep. That newborn baby was kicking his ass if Nic went by his look.

"My baby birds," he teased.

"What the hell ever," she said, melting into his hug. "wasn't nobody following you around."

Ness laughed. "If anything, we were following Marcellus. He was more fun than you anyway."

Damian put a hand on his chest. "Dang, cousin, that hurt."

"Lies," Audrey protested, pulling him into a hug.

He stepped back and assessed them. "Sorry I missed Sunday dinner, I really wanted to see y'all."

Nic waved away his apology, "You have a new baby. We got time to catch up."

"Oh yeah, how long y'all staying?" He raised his brow.

The women shared a look. "I'll be here a while," Nic said vaguely. "I can work from home, so I'm good anywhere."

"Same," Ness chimed in.

They all looked at Audrey. She held up her hands. "I'm taking it a day at a time." Her answer was even vaguer than Nic's.

"Cellus told us you were the man to come see about yummy beers," Ness broke into the awkward silence.

"Bet. I can hook you guys up," he laughed.

"I'll leave you with Damian and go hunt down your Uncle," Aunt Becca said.

They waited until the click of her heels was further down the hallway before speaking.

"Think they're going to hide evidence?" Audrey asked.

Damian groaned. "Cellus got to y'all." He waved for them to follow him. He took them back up front where the bar was.

Audrey shrugged. "I haven't talked to Cellus yet."

"I was going to look before I even talked to Cellus if that makes you feel better," Nic told him.

"It's not healthy, Nic." He went behind the bar.

They each grabbed a stool.

"Healthier than obsessing about it," Nic murmured.

He sighed and put down small glasses. "I'll start you with the pale lager we have."

He poured a little into each of their glasses.

"How many do you make?" Ness asked, smelling hers.

"Right now, just pale and blonde. I'm working on a red; I just can't get the flavor the way I want it." He waited on them to taste.

"You're not the least bit curious?" Nicole ignored hers.

"I'm just as mad as Cellus. I would just rather trust the police to do their jobs." He crossed his arms over his chest.

"How is it going around here? Any rumors?" Audrey asked, sipping from her glass.

"Besides the fact that our grandmother left her company to three women who've never stepped foot inside?" He asked with a smirk.

"Is that what they're saying?" Nic asked.

"There are six employees, so there's not a whole lot of gossip happening," he said, pouring them another glass.

"How does Uncle Brandon feel?" She asked, tensing.

"You could ask your Uncle yourself," a booming voice said behind them.

Nic grimaced and pasted a smile on her face before turning. Despite every woman in their family being petite, their Uncle Brandon managed to nearly reach six feet tall. He was a big man, wide, round shoulders, a slight pooch, and an austere face that belied the fact that he was a gentle man. She smiled and walked over to him. He enveloped her, smelling of cigar smoke and a cologne she could never place. She closed her eyes and gripped him tightly, transported to her childhood for the brief moment in his arms. She backed away and took a beat to assess him. He looked tired.

With her hand on his shoulder, she reached for her power, so unpredictable but always under the surface. Immediately impressions from her Uncle bombarded her and her eyes filled. He was hurting. Guilt, anger, and sorrow all mixed within. Guilt for what, though? He stepped around her, ending her contact, and hugged Audrey.

"Hey, Uncle," Audrey greeted.

He picked up Ness next, and she squealed. He laughed and set her down, sliding his hands in his pockets.

"I hate the why, but I am thrilled you girls are back home," He said. "Becs said you're staying a while?"

Nic nodded. "I forgot how much I love it here."

"That's understandable. Lauren barely left dust behind when she left," He laughed. "You come to check out your inheritance?"

The cousins shared a look.

"The place is impressive. I can't believe what you've accomplished," Nic said.

"Mother came up with the original recipe, but Damian has expounded on it," Brandon told them.

Damian gave them a salute.

"I can't believe Grandmother left it to us when the two of you have been doing the work," Ness said, her hand on his shoulder.

"I know I look young and svelte, but I'm reaching retirement age, and since I don't have any kids, it makes sense," Brandon answered.

Nicole searched his face for any hidden meaning. Finding none, she relaxed.

"When you three are ready, we can go over operations." Brandon wrapped an arm around Ness.

"You're leaving altogether?" Ness asked in surprise.

"I'll make sure y'all know everything you need first, of course," He assured them.

Nic shook her head. "I don't mind knowing the ins and outs, but I love my job and have no plans to leave anytime soon."

Uncle Brandon nodded. Aunt Becca looked relieved.

"Well, then, shall we?" Aunt Becs waved to the door leading to what Nic could only assume were the offices.

They all followed behind her. Nicole had her doubts that she would learn anything helpful on this trip, but she'd keep her eyes open. Perhaps between the three of them, something would click.

Chapter Fourteen

Saturday night was a good night for the bar. It was one of the only ones for at least thirty miles, so everyone living on the outskirts of town made it their regular hang out if they didn't feel like driving way out to the Island clubs. Most of the patrons were the bikers in the area, both human and shifter alike, so it was a rough crowd.

Just his type of people.

JT lined up the shot on the pool table and knocked down another ball. Dante cursed on the other end of the table. They'd been trading insults and talking shit for the past two hours, keeping an eye on the crowd that was slowly gathering in the small bar. He took his time lining up another shot, hoping concentrating on that task would help push thoughts of Nicole from his head. He cursed as he missed the ball.

Just thinking of her name had him all fucked up. Dante laughed and circled the table to take a shot.

"Hey, you hear anything about anyone messing around Ms. Patsy's house?"

Dante straightened and frowned. "Nah, what's going on?"

"I was talking to Nic last night on the phone, and someone tried to break in." He took a sip of his beer, his mind going back to how calmly Nicole had handled that situation.

"It's Nic now, huh," Dante smirked and knocked a ball in the pocket.

"Man, whatever. You heard anything?"

Dante stood up and propped his arm on the top of his pool stick. "I ain't heard nothing, but I'll keep an ear to the ground. Want me to send someone 'round there?"

JT thought on it before shaking his head. "I'll do it."

"Look at you, protecting your woman," Dante taunted.

"Fuck you, Te."

Dante chuckled and then cursed, standing taller. "God damned, the whole lot of them fine as hell."

JT snorted and looked towards the door, already knowing who he was talking about. His wolf perked up and moved through his body. His mouth dried as he saw what Nicole was wearing. The tight black dress stopped mid-thigh and hugged every one of her curves. Her short black leather jacket matched the ass-kicking pair of combat boots she wore and...God damned, that woman knew how to entice. Her skin bared with her every move, and his dick bricked in his pants. She blended in with the rest of his patrons but stood out at the same time. Her hair was up in a bun, and curly tendrils framed her face. She was walking temptation. Someone else next to them cursed, and JT swung his stick, hitting him in the back of the head.

"Watch your eyes, prospect," He growled.

His wolf was already doing the possessive thing, which didn't bode well for him. He needed to talk to his father. He turned and made eye contact with a table full of bikers near the back and nodded towards the women. The men hastily stood, offering their table to Nicole and her cousins. He went back to his game.

No use in him looking thirsty, like the rest of the motherfuckers in here.

On the other hand, Dante didn't even try to disguise it. He stared over at their table hard.

"Damn, Te," he drawled. "You gonna play or make eyes at Ness all night?"

Dante shook his head and went back to the game. "I'm 'bout out of patience with our little cat."

JT snorted and chalked the end of his stick. "Whatever you say."

He continued playing with his cousin, keeping half an eye on their table for the last hour. It wasn't like they were the only women in the club, but he knew the very moment the three of them hit the dance floor. Outside of the whistles and catcalls, lust swelled in the air. His body tightened, and he was almost afraid to turn around.

"Fuck. We gon' have to fight," Dante said, putting his stick down on the table.

"They can handle themselves," he assured his cousin.

He made the mistake of turning around, though. And yeah...they were gonna have to fight some bold motherfucker tonight. JT crossed his arms over his chest and watched the three women. They were all stunning and looked enough alike that anyone would think they were sisters. He'd grown up with Ness, so he damn near considered her a sister. She wore a pair of leather shorts and a wife-beater beneath the leather coat she wore. Her boots reached the top of her knees, and he understood why Dante was drooling next to him.

He wasn't as close to Audrey as he was Ness, but still, there was no lust as he skimmed the tight black jeans she wore with a cut-off t-shirt. She was as sexy as the other two, though there was a dangerous air around her that kept JT's wolf on alert. There had been many times he'd witnessed a young Audrey coming into this same bar to pull her drunk mother out. Back in those days, the bar had been rougher, unquestionably no place for a little girl. He imagined she'd seen some shit growing up, so he respected her 'take no shit' attitude. He shook his head as she mushed a man who'd gotten too close to her.

There was something about Nicole, though. His eyes went back to her. Something that called to him and his wolf. Lord, that woman moved like a song. Sexy, her hips moving to a sound that was all heavy drums and yearning guitar riffs. It was no wonder he couldn't take his eyes off of her.

He watched her dance for another half hour, his dick hard and straining against his fatigue pants. They were all a siren song, and it left no question as to how the Fouche women bespelled men. Periodically, Nic would lift her eyes and meet his. It took everything in him to keep his wolf from answering her call. If he were a sane man, he'd back away and leave her be. The Fouches weren't a family to be trifled with, especially for a man intent to live out his natural life. Even pushing rumors aside, there were concrete stories of the chaos that followed in the family's wake. Still, his wolf could give a shit. It brushed against his skin, anxious, determined.

Any intelligent person would resist temptation.

JT showed his canines as yet another dumbass sidled up to the women. His growl carried over the sound of the music, and the male's head whipped up as he scanned the room. His eyes landed on JT. Hands in the air, the male nodded at JT and walked away. Nicole's gaze met his, and her eyes went wide. She licked her lips, and JT's dick jumped in response. What was that about resisting? The longer she stared and moved her hips, the further back into the recesses of his mind that thought drifted. Lord have mercy, she was sexy as hell.

He made his way to her, unable to stay away a moment longer. He slid up behind her, grabbing her hips. She threw her arms up and smiled over her shoulder.

"About time," she taunted.

He leaned over her neck and inhaled her scent. Heady, deep and rich, her smell warmed his body and dragged his wolf forward. They danced as though they were the only two on the floor. For him, the rest of the world fell away. Her hips swaying had his undivided attention. He turned her so that her back was to his front and dragged his teeth down her neck.

"I've been thinking about you all day," he admitted.

He slid his hand up the soft skin of her leg, and she shuddered, her breath bathing his cheek as he tipped her chin towards him. He kissed her, unable to resist the temptation of her full painted lips. The sweet taste of her exploded on his tongue, and he growled, minutes from giving his wolf control.

She pulled back and gave him a smile that was pure seduction. "We should leave and go to your place."

He could definitely get with that. "I'm right upstairs."

She spun in his arms and went up on her toes, "Even better."

The kiss she gave him blew the top of his head off, and he gripped her ass in his hands.

"Let me let the girls know where I'm going," she whispered.

He nodded and walked to the bar. Emily slid him a shot with a smirk. He downed it in one gulp, the heat making it worse. JT watched her talk to her cousins, shaking his head at the knowing smiles they gave him. They turned back to dancing, spinning up the lust in the room. He'd leave Dante to handle that. Hopefully, there wouldn't be a bar brawl before the end of the night. Her hips swayed as she walked to him and his mouth dried.

He gripped her waist when she was close enough and pulled her into his chest. "You sure about this?"

"Absolutely," she whispered.

He leaned down and devoured her mouth, impatience riding him. He pulled back and damn near dragged her down the back hallway and up the stairs to his apartment. He pulled her inside and locked the door, pushing her against it.

"Lord have mercy," he whispered and dipped down to taste her again.

Chapter Fifteen

JT was on her from the moment he closed the door to his apartment. The music from downstairs was thumping through the walls, the bass pumping through her blood. Her cat was rising. She only prayed the wild magic didn't slip out of her control. JT kissed her, their tongues battling for control. His wolf was on the surface, a pressure pushing against her power. It was a heady feeling.

He trailed wet, open-mouth kisses down her neck. He nudged the collar of her dress aside with his chin, scraping his teeth against her collar bone. She closed her eyes and threw her head back. His kisses wandered further down her body, his hands lifting her skirt. She helped him, pulling it up around her waist.

"Open your legs to me," he demanded.

The slow, rough drawl of his accent had her obeying instantly. He rewarded her for it, kneeling, his tongue lashing against the folds of her sex.

"Oh fuck," she whispered, opening her legs wider.

JT devoured her, his tongue circling her clit, rubbing against it hard enough for her to see stars. She propped her leg over his shoulder, and she was lost. Nicole had been fantasizing about him all night, so her body was primed for his touch. It took nothing for her to crash over the edge. He nipped her thigh before setting her leg back on the ground. He rose over her, his body pressing against hers. He licked across her lips, demanding entry into her mouth.

She obliged him, sinking into the kiss. He pulled back, and his eyes glowed, the wolf inside him staring back at her. Her power rose to meet it, and she sucked in a breath at the force of it.

"On your knees," he demanded softly.

She dropped quickly, impatient to taste him. She fumbled with his pants, pulling down the zipper and gripping his dick. There was no foreplay, no teasing. She took him deep into her mouth, grinning at his answering groan. It pushed her arousal higher. He gripped her hair, holding her in place, and watched her, his breath hissing out as she swallowed him down. She looked up, and at that moment, her cat pushed forward, trapping him in her gaze. His eyes lost focus, flashing back and forth with his wolf. The lust in his thoughts washed over her, and she shivered in anticipation.

"Fuck," he cursed, breaking eye contact and pulling from her mouth. "You're dangerous," he muttered, whipping her around.

She rested her face against the cool wall and smiled, knowing that she had him exactly where she wanted him. She heard the condom wrapper rip open, and she went to her toes.

JT cursed because, God damn, this woman would take his soul if he wasn't careful. The power of her cat had drawn both he and his wolf into her. He'd nearly lost himself in her eyes. She turned her head back to glance at him, her hips winding. He gripped her waist and slammed himself home. The music's bass seemed to surround him, the driving beat matching the rhythm of his heartbeat. She reached back and scraped her nails up his legs, and he growled. He liked that shit.

He grabbed her breasts, pinching her nipples, and pumped into her, his strokes hard and deep as fuck. Nic pulled his hand up and put it to the front of her neck.

Submission.

Yeah, her cat knew who the fuck she belonged to. He growled and squeezed her throat, speeding his strokes. She moaned, working her hips against him. He nudged her chin around to him and kissed her, plunging his tongue into her mouth. She nipped his tongue with her teeth, giving back as good as she got. It was like she was made for him, his roughness.

That kind of thinking was dangerous, so instead of letting those thoughts intrude, he pushed deeper, holding her hips in place so she would take every inch. She did so without flinching, her moans getting louder with his every thrust. He felt his climax looming, a tingle working its way up his spine. He released her neck and reached down to her clit. He circled it once, twice before pinching it. She went careening into an orgasm, her spasming channel pulling him down with her. Her scream stroked his ego, and he pushed in one final time before he came. He was breathing hard as his body tremored with aftershocks.

"My God," she whispered with a husky laugh. "You backed your shit-talking up."

He laughed, leaning on her back. She glanced over her shoulder, her smile sensual and telling of a woman well satisfied. He would like to think he was too cool for that shit to matter, but he had to admit it stroked over his ego. He kissed her shoulder and pulled out. She turned and wrapped her arms around his shoulder.

"I know you don't think I'm done with you," she purred.

He lifted her. "Oh, I plan to wear your ass out, don't worry."

She laughed and wrapped her legs around his waist. "You do understand that this can't be anything other than what it is, right?"

"You don't want strings. I'm with that," JT assured her, carrying her to his bedroom. "Don't even worry about it."

Nicole was by no means a virgin, by anyone's standards. She, like her mama, loved men and women all across the spectrum. Sex was a great stress relief, and she partook when she could. Sex with JT, though…

Shit.

Sex with JT had her reconsidering some things. It was about round three when she realized she'd bitten off more than she could chew. Her emotions were trying to get tangled up, and that was never a good thing. Unlike her mother, she did not need a husband, one nor five. She sighed as JT slid a hand across her stomach.

"I can see the wheels spinning, Fouche," he murmured in a sleepy voice that made her body parts tingle.

She traced the tattoos on his arm. "You have so many tattoos. Do any of them have meaning?"

He snickered, seeing through her diversion tactic. "They all mean something to me."

"That's not an answer," she chided.

"Most of them are for protection. Some of them are just art I really liked."

She turned and faced him, propping her head on her hand. "Protection from what?"

"All manner of things, Fouche," he said softly, nibbling on her chin.

"Like what?"

He nuzzled into her neck, his hands drifting down to her sex. She opened her legs, obliging him. "It keeps practitioners and witches from calling my animal. Protection, Nic, nothing deep."

She hissed as he rubbed against her clit. "That sounds deep to me."

"You talking way too much for me," he said before melding their mouths together.

"Your work is hazardous," she commented when he pulled back.

JT sighed and moved his hand from between his legs. "Is that what you're gonna use?"

"I'm not..." she paused because he was right. She was looking for excuses.

"Let it be fun for now, Fouche, quit scaring yourself," he murmured against her lips. "I thought we both agreed there would be no strings."

She nodded. He was right. She'd agreed to that very thing, not more than a few hours ago. So why was she tripping? "I need to go."

"You gon' run from this, Nic?"

Her eyes traced his face. "It might be safer for you if I did."

"Something about me say I'm scary?"

"Maybe I'm the scary one," she whispered.

"Bullshit. Fouche women are made of steel."

She gave him a small chuckle and got up. "Where are my clothes?"

"Many places," he said smugly, leaning back against his headboard.

She snorted and went on the hunt. He entered the living room as she was sliding her dress up her legs. He pulled her into his arms and kissed her deeply. Fuck, she could be in trouble with this man.

"I like you a lot Jeremiah Taylor," She whispered against his lips.

"Come on. I'll drive you home."

She tucked her underwear into her jacket pocket and followed him downstairs. She knew leaving was the right thing to do, but watching his swagger, knowing what he was toting between his legs... It was hard not just to say fuck it and go back upstairs. But, some distance would be prudent. She was due another pep talk. Her last name might be Oliver, but she was a Fouche, and it was vital that she not forget that.

Chapter Sixteen

Nicole had barely stepped out of the shower when the doorbell rang. She ignored it, knowing one of the others would answer. She was sliding her blankets back, ready to get into bed, when she heard her name called out. Growling, she went to the door of her bedroom.

"Yeah?"

"TiTi Shelby's here," Ness called up.

Nic frowned and quickly slid on some shorts. She was down the stairs moments later, staring at her aunt in surprise. Shelby carried a wicker basket in her hands and a canvas bag over her shoulder.

"What's going on, Titi?" Nic asked, taking the basket from her.

"Thank you, love." Shelby kissed her cheek. "The streets are buzzing, niece," was all she said as she passed her three nieces and headed down the hallway.

Nic shared a look with her cousins before they all filed behind their aunt. Shelby stopped in the room their grandmother kept in the back and used a workshop. Audrey rushed past her and picked up the stuff she had scattered across the room.

"Sorry, it's messy," Audrey muttered.

Shelby smiled. "I'm glad you're using it."

She spread the ingredients from her bag onto the table. Nic picked up the empty Mason jar and frowned, her curiosity aroused. There were seeds, some kind of wood chips in separate little piles. Ness picked up the powder and held it to her nose.

"Girl, you know better than that," Aunt Shelby gently chastised, taking the small baggy from Ness.

"What are we doing?" Audrey's eyes were taking it all in, excitement circling her.

Nic put down the jar and awaited the answer, very curious.

"Well, as I said, talk is going around town," Shelby started.

"About what?" Nic asked.

"About you, love." Shelby smiled and raised her eyebrows.

"Oop, business all in the street," Ness said, cackling

"This town is too damn small," Nic muttered.

Ness kept laughing. "I told you that last night."

Nic sighed because Ness had warned her last night that everyone would know if she slept with JT. She couldn't believe it happened so fast. Her cheeks heated. She had no desire to talk about sex with her aunt. Audrey laughed and helped Shelby pull out more stuff.

Shelby turned her eyes to Nic. "I know you girls scoff at the family curse, but as I've experienced it first hand, I came to offer a bit of help."

Nicole shook her head. She definitely didn't scoff at the curse that followed behind her mother's every marriage.

"What kind of help?" Nic squinted at the basket.

"A protection spell for your boo."

"He's not my...we're not serious or anything." She stopped short of telling her aunt she was riding JT for sport.

Audrey snickered, seeming to read her mind.

"All the same and just in case," Shelby said. She filled the jar with the clear liquid halfway. "Grind these," she ordered Audrey.

Audrey pulled out a mortar and pestle and ground the seed as her aunt ordered.

"No offense TiTi, but this hasn't seemed to work in our family," Ness said softly.

Shelby gave a sad smile. "I had fifteen years with the love of my life. It works well enough."

Nic touched her aunt's shoulder.

Shelby sighed and shook her head, "none of that. Our minds have to be in the right place for this to be effective. Nic, you need to be the one to prepare this."

"Why do you think it stopped working with Uncle Lucian?" Nic asked, taking the jar her aunt offered.

"Honestly, I've always been of a mind that something else... someone else worked harder to make sure it didn't work," Shelby said, passing her the wood chips.

Nic got a chill. She scooped up the tiny bits of wood. "What is this?"

"Black snakeroot," Shelby said absently, flipping through an aged book.

"You think someone is still after our family?" Audrey asked, frowning.

Shelby shrugged. "Not that me or mama could prove it."

She shared a look with her cousins. Could it have something to do with their Grandmother's death?

"Why hasn't anyone tried to break the spell," Ness asked, leaning over the table to read the book.

Shelby snorted. "As you all know, your mothers each had their own ideas about the curse and what to do about it."

Nic thought of all the years her mother ran and was still trying to outrun their family name.

"Mama had more power than all of us combined. If she couldn't do it, no way, four bickering sisters could." Shelby sounded resigned. "And after I lost Lucian, I just...I couldn't think of a reason to go through the trouble. I'm sorry to say."

"I've only gotten bits and pieces of what the curse is over the years. Can you explain what started it?" Nicole asked. If any of them had a chance to break the curse, she needed to understand it better.

They got quiet, and Nic added the ingredients as her aunt passed them to her.

"It started with my great grandmother, I think. It's been so long since I've talked about it," Aunt Shelby finally broke the silence. "According to our family's side of things. A man named Henry had fallen for Rose, our ancestor. The story gets fuzzy on whether or not they were involved in any type of relationship, but Rose met our great-grandfather Montrose and fell in love with him. Henry was distraught, and after trying to get Rose back and failing, he killed himself. His family—powerful practitioners from how mama told it—were angry. They punished Rose, and Montrose was the first victim of the curse."

"My God," Ness said. "What are the specifics of the curse?"

Aunt Shelby sighed. "According to family legend, the women were cursed to lose anyone they loved romantically because Rose rejected Henry. It varies, I guess, depending on which sister tells the story. Mama said they would die, but my Aunt Liz said they would leave. I've seen both happen within our own family, so I assume them both to be true."

"And the cat?" Nic asked.

This time Shelby chuckled and shook her head. "The cat was Rose's punishment for 'catting around town.' Such a stupid saying. Either way, we shift into pumas every full moon, at least the women do."

"Does the curse keep us from controlling it?" That was the real question Nic wanted to be answered.

"Oh, sweetie," Shelby cupped her cheek. "Lauren sheltered you from so much. In her haste to escape the curse, she refused to train you. Mama taught us how to control the cat's magic enough to keep it from running our lives. We don't have any control over the shifting. It happens like clockwork on the full moon, but I'm sure you've experienced the other power that comes with it. Keeping that power contained takes a lot of work."

"Hell yeah, it does," Ness muttered. "Without the Taylors, I would've been attacking people up and down the east coast."

"So, with training, we can get that part of ourselves under control?" Nic pressed.

Shelby studied her, her magic prodding Nicole. Her cat responded quickly, power rising and filling the room. Her aunt smiled and raised an eyebrow.

"Interesting," was all she said. "Now, back to the task at hand. You'll need to redo this in another year, you know, if you last that long." She gave her niece a sly look that told Nicole she didn't believe her words that their relationship was temporary. "Right now, these ingredients reflect the age of your relationship. The longer you last, the more aged you'll want your ingredients."

"TiTi," Nicole said softly, squelching the longing in her voice.

Shelby ignored the warning. "As you pour into the jar, breathe and set your intentions with Spirit."

Nic did as ordered, carefully adding each ingredient to the jar. Though she had no far-reaching intentions with JT, she didn't want him hurt from their family's curse. She slowed her breathing the way her mentor had taught her and said a quick prayer.

"Seal the jar," Shelby ordered, observing her. "You need to take this to JT and put it someplace no one will bother with it."

"Without his knowledge?" Nic was surprised.

"No, love. Make sure he knows and knows not to bother with it." Aunt Shelby said with a chuckle.

"Honestly, Aunt Shelby, I don't think we're this far into a relationship that I want to bring up protection spells," she said flippantly.

"JT been coming to mama for years for protection spells. He probably won't even blink at this."

"What do you mean?" Ness asked.

"Half them tattoos on that wolf's body were designed by mama. Especially after he became Alpha of the Taylor pack."

Nicole's eyebrows skyrocketed. "So he and Grandmother were close?"

"This family and the Taylor family have worked together to protect this town longer than even I can remember. Mama took care of the Taylor Alphas my whole life. She did have a soft spot for JT, though."

Nic frowned. That was shocking. Intriguing...but shocking. He hadn't really said anything to her about how close he worked with her grandmother. Not that he would, given she purposely kept their conversations light and limited. And to now give him a protection spell...She imagined JT would read a lot more into it than she wanted him to.

Aunt Shelby sighed. "I leave it up to you, Nic. But, if you have any feelings for him, I would ask that you consider it."

They stared each other down. Shelby's empathy and worry reached out to her, and Nicole finally nodded.

Shelby smiled. "Great. I have to go pick up my grandbabies."

Their aunt gathered her items and put them carefully back into her bag. Nic and her cousins followed her to the front door and waved as she drove off.

"What are you going to do?" Ness asked.

Nic sighed. "I don't know. It's a little soon to be giving him protection spells. It feels like trying to claim him."

Audrey snickered. "JT is mired in this world. I don't think he'll think anything of it."

"Mired?" Ness shook her head. "You and your fancy boarding school words."

"Excuse you. I didn't go to boarding school." Audrey sucked her teeth. "And how in the world do you manage to make it sound like an insult?"

"It's a skill," Ness said, walking off.

Nic laughed at their antics and sobered quickly. JT's job was already dangerous enough, would messing around with her make it worse? Her eyes drifted down the hall towards her grandmother's workshop. What was stopping her from giving him the protection spell? Pride, a little ego?

Chapter Seventeen

JT crossed his arms over his chest, chilling against the wall as the driver pulled two kegs out of the back of his van. It was Monday, and he had a few different deliveries on the way. This current one was legal, so he was relaxed, though he still kept an eye on his surroundings. He eyed the Springbrook logo on the side of the van and thought back to his conversation with Nic. How far had she gotten with her investigation? Because he was stalled. He was debating what his next move should be. He'd told Cellus to follow the money, and it was generally good advice.

He'd discreetly asked around about it within contacts he had. None of the witches or practitioners had known anything about enemies Patsy had made. She'd been highly regarded in the magical community, so everyone he'd asked had been as puzzled as he. He was still working his way through the shifters, though that felt like a dead end. Most shifters avoided magic users in general and most especially the powerful ones.

He hoped Nicole and her cousins had had better luck. He pulled out his phone since she was on his mind.

JT: What you up to Fouche?

He watched the dots start and then stop before starting again. He smiled. Was she gonna cuss him out or answer his question?

Fouche: Working.

He snorted at the short answer.

JT: Come see me when you get off.

He hadn't intended to say that, but now that it was out, he waited on her answer.

Fouche: People are already talking.

JT: Ion care about 'people.'

"I'm done, JT," the driver called out.

JT tucked his phone in his back pocket and signed his name at the bottom of the clipboard.

"How is it going over there? I heard the granddaughters were supposed to be taking over." It wasn't his business, but curiosity propelled him to ask.

The driver shrugged. "Supposedly. We haven't had any changes yet, though, so I don't know."

JT grunted.

"I heard they came by the other day when the plant was closed." The driver added. "I also heard they fine as hell."

JT smiled and pushed down on his wolf because the man wasn't exactly disrespectful. Nic was fine, and he was just speaking facts.

"What happened when they came by?"

"No one knows, but Mr. Fouche showed up to work, as usual, this morning." He climbed up into his truck. "I'll see you next week."

JT waved and went back inside. His back pocket buzzed finally, and he smiled.

Fouche: fine

JT: So loquacious

Fouche: now spell it without spellcheck.

Her mean ass.

He busted out laughing. He sat down at his desk and spotted a sticky note. It was in Dante's sloppy scrawl. It had Wulfen and a phone number scribbled. What did that even mean? His phone vibrated across his desk. He frowned at the private number.

"Yeah?"

"JT, it's Jedidiah."

JTs wolf sat up at the man's power. "Jedidiah."

"I got a problem." Jedidiah's voice was gruff. It always made the old man sound aggressive, which aided in the many stories about him.

JT bristled at the tone. "Now, Jed, you know how I roll. You may be able to call all manner of wolves to you, but Taylor wolves don't belong to you, nor do we work for you."

"I think you'll want to help me with my problem." The power in the man's tone washed over him.

JT growled because Jedidiah tried to take his mind even knowing he was protected. "Now I definitely ain't doing shit for you."

"Patsy's gone. Who you think will protect you now?" Jed snapped.

"Not you thinking Ms. Patsy would leave me ass out."

He fingered the bracelet she had given him when he'd seen her last. It had been a couple of weeks before her death. Ms. Patsy had told him as long as a Fouche lived on that land, his wolves would be protected. He, in turn, had renewed his pack's promise to protect her family's land as a part of their territory. It was a deal that had been in place for generations, and as the Alpha of the Taylor Pack, he hadn't hesitated to keep up their families' alliance.

"I heard her granddaughters are settling into her place," Jedidiah said casually.

Interesting that Jed would hear that as far out as Northern Georgia. Why would that be news to anyone outside of this town? JT thought about the strange scents around Ms. Patsy's property. He'd told Nicole about the scents, but he'd left out that he could smell magic behind it. Could Jedidiah be involved? He would need to look into it.

"Did you call about something specific, Jedidiah, or are you calling to test your powers now that Ms. Patsy's gone?"

"I want my supplies from you," Jed said reluctantly.

JT leaned back in his chair. "Is that right? I thought you didn't need my mangy pack."

"That silly boy who took over the Wulfen has no idea what he's doing."

The Wulfen was under new 'management'? Now, JT didn't know that. He looked down at the note Dante had left on his desk. Was it the number for the new leader? He didn't deal with the Wulfen. They were impulsive and young as hell. Two things that would get a wolf killed when dealing with magic wielders.

He grunted, waiting for Jedidiah to get to the point.

"I've left your wolves alone."

"Except when you haven't," JT drawled. "Last time I caught you trying to manipulate a wolf of mine, do you remember what happened, Jedidiah?"

"You cut me off," the other man growled, surly.

"Now, say I start back supplying you. I want a guarantee this time, written in blood. I'm not finna be going back and forth with you every time you decide to test new magic."

The other line was silent, the man digesting JT's ultimatum.

"Fine, deal."

"Text me your order. I'll deliver it myself and get this promise out in writing."

The other man hissed and hung up. JT put down his phone, picked the sticky note again, and tapped it. His sister heard the Wulfen was looking for product to move, and now new management, he wondered if one had to do with the other.

He dialed up Dante.

"Yeah, Cuz."

"This note you left me?"

Dante sucked his teeth. "Yeah, got that call early this morning. Talking about they want to set up a meet."

"Just heard from a client that they're under new management," JT commented.

"Is that right?" Dante hummed. "That does change things a bit."

"That's what I'm thinking. You ain't heard nothing yet?"

"Not yet. It must've been smooth as hell to take over and it not reach the right people," Dante said thoughtfully.

"You feel me? See what you can find out."

"Will do," Dante promised.

"JT," Emily called out.

"I gotta go." He lifted out of his seat and walked to his door. "Yeah?"

"Unc wanna see you," she told him.

He nodded and followed her down the hallway towards the bar. His uncle Earl was sipping at his favorite whisky, talking shit with his father. The two men, though well into their sixties, maybe looked forty. Their wolves were still strong, and their power filled the space around them. They both sat at the bar, their camouflage chest waders hanging around their waist with long-sleeved t-shirts rolled to their elbows. He shook his head at the bucket hats on his bar top. Ain't no telling what the hell they'd been up to.

JT smiled and dapped his dad. "Hey, Unc."

"Nephew!" His Uncle Earl thundered, giving him dap.

"Y'all must be hiding from mama if you in here day drinking."

His dad rolled his eyes. "Trying to get us to go to bible study like we don't have better things to do."

"I hope Auntie Val praying extra hard for all both of y'all," Emily said, filling his dad's glass.

"You was my favorite niece," Will said, shaking his head. "I can't believe you'd do me like that."

Emily snorted and moved on.

"What you got for me, Unc?"

"Went out crabbing the other day with this joker here," Earl told him.

JT snickered. "New boat treating you right, then?"

Earl smiled and tipped back his drink. "Val and Cheryl can hang it up because me and my boy finna stay gone."

He had to laugh because he'd gotten around to seeing that sorry excuse for a boat his Uncle was proud of. And hater his auntie Cheryl may be, she was right about the size of that raft. But, seeing as how his uncle and father looked like they were having the time of their lives, he would keep his opinions to himself.

"Anyway, caught someone out by your stash," Will said casually.

JT stiffened. "Is that right?"

"No worries. Me and Will took care of him," Earl promised. "But then, funny thing he said as my brother's wolf was tearing into him."

JT squinted. "Yeah?"

"Said he was with the Wulfen, and the new boss sent him down, 'just checking the lay of the land.'" Earl put up air quotes.

JT grunted. "I got a message that they wanted to meet. What did he say about this new leader?"

"Came down from Atlanta," Earl said.

"Came down or got run out of town is the question," Will spoke up.

"What you do with the scout?" He wanted to question the man himself.

His dad and uncle shared a look, and JT figured that was that. His father and uncle were both old school. They didn't leave problems to come back up and surprise them. He swallowed his sigh. It was going to make any conversation with the new leader hard. It couldn't be helped in this case.

Will slid him a piece of paper. "All the info we could get out of him."

"My man," JT said, pocketing the information.

"Other than that, you good?" His father asked.

"Jed scurried back," he said.

Earl cussed and touched the cross dangling off his gold chain. "I don't have to tell you—"

JT cut him off. "I told him we weren't dealing with him without paperwork."

Will nodded, his eyes lit with respect. "You think he'll do it?"

It was a big thing to ask a rootworker to sign a contract of any type, especially since the 'paperwork' in this instance would be sealed in blood. He wouldn't deal with the old man unless he'd extracted his promise to leave his wolves alone. Now that Jedidiah understood that he couldn't get decent supplies from anyone but JT, it would be easy.

"Whoever took over for them boys don't have access to the supplies Jed needs, and from the sound of it ain't easy to deal with." JT shrugged. "I'm thinking paperwork won't be too hard to obtain."

"We taught you well," Earl said.

"What else going on?" Will asked, a mischievous glint in his eyes.

Lord, his mama talked too much. She called him after church just yesterday to tell him she heard he and Nic were messing around.

"What she say?" He asked aloud.

Earl laughed, and his father slapped his brother's back, amused.

"She heard you had a Fouche slipping out your back door in the early morning," Will told him.

"The Fouches fine, but if you value a drama-free life, you'll leave that alone," Earl added.

JT and Will both gave him an incredulous look.

"I know you ain't talking," Will said.

The rest of the bar cackled, proof that their conversation wasn't in the least bit private.

"Hey, fuck y'all. My wife is a delicate flower." Earl shouted.

"If she a flower, she a goddamned Venus flytrap," someone called out.

The bar roared, and JT turned his head to keep his uncle from seeing his smile. His brother did no such thing. Will laughed as loud as the rest of them.

"Any-damn-way!" Earl hollered. "Just be careful, nephew."

"Ain't I always," JT answered.

"My boy." His father held up his glass in a toast.

"But, if ever there was a woman tempting enough..." someone called out.

"Watch your mouth," JT growled, and instead of being intimidated, the patrons laughed.

"Oh, he got it bad bad." Someone else said.

"We'll leave you and your tenderoni alone," Will said.

"Oh my God, she's not young," JT protested.

"She tiny, though," Earl said.

JT rolled his eyes and headed back towards his office. "I'll catch y'all later. Please don't make me call mama or Auntie Cheryl."

"See how you do us," Earl called out to his back.

Emily snorted. "Dante told me to text him when they were ready to go home. He coming by to get them."

He smiled at his cousin and went back into his office.

The conversation had his mind on Nicole, though, and now she was all he could think about when he had work shit to deal with. Memories of Saturday night played through his head, and he adjusted as he sat down at his desk. JT smiled. She was coming by tonight, and he couldn't wait.

Chapter Eighteen

Nic adjusted the dress shirt she wore over some warm leggings and hoped no one saw her sneaking up the back stairs to JT's apartment. She told him she'd be over after work, but she'd stalled until it was late enough for no one to see her. She thought about Aunt Shelby's visit and shook her head. It was probably useless to try and sneak around, but she didn't want the county discussing her sex life.

Her thoughts went to the jar she'd left on her bedside table, and guilt prodded her. After hearing the explanation of the curse, it felt reckless not to give JT the jar. She could admit that she purposely left it to prove to herself that she was capable of keeping their relationship to just sex. Gossip aside, it was also the reason she came over to his apartment so late. In the end, keeping their relationship shallow probably protected him more than the jar could.

Right.

Perfectly logical.

Shaking thoughts of the jar and the curse from her head, she took a deep breath and knocked.

JT answered the door shirtless, a pair of jogging pants hanging off his waist. His shoulders were still wet from his shower, and now so was she. His heated gaze roamed her body, his head tilting to the side as his eyes slid down her legs. He gathered her into a hug, and she inhaled, getting drunk off of his scent. There was something about his smell that she loved. He pulled her into the apartment without a word. Their hands clasped, he guided her to the small island separating his kitchen from the living room.

"Want a drink, Fouche?"

No, she didn't want a drink, she came for the dick, but she nodded anyway. He gave her an amused look and opened his fridge, passing her a hard cider. What was so damn funny? Was he making her wait to pay her back for taking so long to come over?

She growled and set her drink on the counter. "What is so amusing?"

He smiled, and butterflies took off in her chest. "Just having a drink with you, Fouche. Otherwise, this would feel like a booty call."

She snorted and took a drink. "Does that satisfy propriety?"

His smirk made her hotter, don't ask her why. She squirmed on her stool. He took a deep inhale, the smile dropping from his face. He growled, and the sound went through her, raising the hair on her arms. She slammed the bottle down on the counter and rounded the corner of the island, pulling his head down into a kiss. He gripped her butt, lifting her and wrapping her legs around his waist. They deepened the kiss, and she moaned as all the giddy excitement she'd been suppressing all day welled inside. He backed them up and lifted her to his countertop, his eyes bright with the presence of his wolf.

He parted her legs and stepped back, dragging her pants and underwear with him. The hungry sound that left his throat went down her spine, and she arched her back, panting. JT gripped her thighs and lowered his head. She grabbed the side of his head, and her power overcame her. She fell into his gaze, seeing visions of them in the bed, rolling around on the sheets. It ramped up her arousal, scorching through her system. She could feel him inside her mind. His excitement, his hunger...all of it. She released a moan.

JT chuckled and nipped across her thighs, his teeth scraping against her skin. Her clit beat a heavy rhythm, matching her racing heartbeat. JT moved closer, his warm breath brushing across her sex, sending shivers down her spine. She was ready to beg at this point. She didn't have to because he licked across the lips of her pussy and then went to work. She threw her head back, first relaxing into the pleasure. She released the breath she'd been holding, and her muscles loosened in relief. She'd been tense with anticipation since he called her, and for every flicker of his tongue, that tension left her body. Soon though, under his expertise, her body tightened again, this time a looming orgasm sending electricity down her skin. She made the mistake of looking down, seeing the pleasure on his face as he ate her, and she fell apart.

JT gave her no time to recover. He sheathed his dick in a condom and pushed inside. He rode her, his face a mask of concentration. Their eyes met, and the rest of the room dropped from her sight. It was just the two of them in a cocoon of pleasure. The only sound was their rapid breathing. JT licked along the column of her neck.

"My God, you tempt me to want things we're not ready for," he rasped against her skin.

She knew what he meant and understood that anything else would be a gamble though they could share this pleasure. With every push of his hips, temptation rose.

"Fuck, you feel amazing," he panted.

"More, JT," she whispered. It spurred him on, and his hips punched into her.

Nic gritted her teeth as her power started to rise, her cat demanding to take over. Her body bucked as JT stroked into her. She went up into flames, her struggle with her cat forgotten as another blinding orgasm swept through her body. He stood over her, and they locked eyes. Her power rolled over them both, and JT growled, his wolf's power pushing against hers.

"Your room, now," she demanded.

He lifted her roughly, his eyes glowing but not leaving hers. He fought against her power, pushing her against the wall next to his bedroom door. He entered her again, and she hissed as he filled her, pressing against her clenching muscles.

"You and your cat will learn better than to play with me, Fouche," he growled, pulling out and slamming back into her.

Her eyes crossed, and she knew a couple more of those strokes would send her over the edge for the third time. JT pushed into her again, his teeth scraping down her neck. He fucked her against the wall, every stroke sending fire racing down her back.

"You know what the fuck I want. Give it to me," he gritted out, powering into Nic.

Her cat protested, her power filling her chest. He chuckled when she gripped his shoulder, her nails digging into her skin.

"Oh, I don't mind the fight, kitten."

His wolf rubbed against her, and she lost it, her stomach clenching, her pussy clamping down onto him. The temptation to lift her chin and expose her neck to this man had her body shaking. Her cat was fighting alongside her, for once, the two of them in some type of tacit agreement. She locked her legs around his waist and gritted her teeth to keep another orgasm at bay. Her eyes sprang open as he moved them, moving in and out of her as he walked towards his bedroom. He turned and sat on the edge of the bed, bringing her into his lap.

She unlocked her legs and pressed her knees down on the bed. Sweat was dripping from them both, and JT was straining to keep it together.

Oh, that won't do. Nic arched her back to take him deeper, allowing her power to fill her and sweep over them both.

He closed his eyes tight. "Fuck, Nicole, I can feel your cat. She's a mean little thing."

When he opened his eyes, they were glowing with his wolf. It was apparent they both liked it. She rode him, bouncing up and down on his dick. He spurred her on, gripping her hair and pulling her head back, forcing the submission she held back from him. He sucked on her neck, licking across her pulse.

"Almost there," he panted, lifting his hips to go deeper.

She cupped his cheeks, demanding his attention. Once he looked at her, she let loose her power, pulling him into the sensual vortex going through her body. His eyes widened, and his hips lost their rhythm as he desperately pumped into her. They both came, Nic screaming his name as wave after wave of pleasure sucked her under. He pulled them both down onto the bed, and she collapsed, panting onto his chest. She had no plans to stay the night, but damn if she would be able to move for a while.

JT tensed as something woke him. He'd been sleeping hard, the satisfying feel of her in his arms settling him into sleep. His wolf woke him, and though he kept his eyes closed, his body was alert for whatever danger his wolf sensed. Nicole stiffened in his arms, and he understood it not to be a physical danger but danger of a whole other nature. One was that was definitely scarier. Nicole was pulling away, no doubt trying to escape and leave. His wolf whined and pressed against his skin, urging him to mark her.

He pulled her closer into him and nuzzled into her neck. She sighed, settling into his body. He nipped her skin and slid his legs between hers, separating her thighs. The heat of her sex radiated out, waking his dick. He desperately wanted to push in, but though he was gone off her, he wasn't that far gone. Even if she had a cat she couldn't control, she wasn't a shifter in the same sense as him and probably could get pregnant without a heat. He leaned back and fumbled on the bedside table until his hand clutched a condom.

She reached down between her legs and gripped him. He hissed and closed his eyes. Would he ever get enough of her? He slid on the condom and pushed into her wet heat. Hell no, that didn't seem possible. At least not for a little while longer. He understood that falling for her wasn't in the cards, despite what his wolf was urging him to do. He needed to be smart about the whole thing. He stroked in and out of her, a feeling he was too scared to name filling his chest. No, it wasn't possible that he could get enough of her.

He clutched her tight to his chest, his strokes leisurely as he savored the scorching clasp of her pussy. Given the option, he would stay there all morning, but she tightened down on him, and JT exploded. Nic wasn't far behind him, her long moan mirroring his. He dropped kisses along her damp skin as they came down from their orgasm. He tightened his hold, wanting to sink further into her.

"I can't stay the night, JT." She blurted.

He growled in irritation. "I know, Nicole."

She turned and faced him. "Well, technically, I did stay the night; it's morning."

He peered at the clock and snorted. It was precisely two in the morning.

She smiled and cupped his cheek. "If ever there were a man who could make me forget..." she trailed off.

He leaned down and devoured her mouth. They were panting when he pulled back.

"Don't make promises my wolf won't understand." Even now, the animal was pushing against him, furious that she would leave their bed. He rolled over and left the bed, wanting to be the first one to pull away. A petty point, but all the same...

He brought back a wet cloth, and she was staring at him as he cleaned her. It was the least he could do to calm his wolf. He finished, tossed it aside, and crawled up her body.

"Text me when you get home, Fouche."

She nodded, kissed him lightly. "Why do you insist on calling me that?"

His eyes traced her face. "It's a reminder of what's at stake." Lord knows he needed that reminder.

Nic sobered and rolled from the bed. He didn't bother pulling on clothes as he walked her to the front door. She turned on the front step, opened her mouth, but then seemed to change her mind, simply waving and heading for her jeep.

Chapter Nineteen

S hit happens. It was a well-known fact. As dangerous as JT's job was, he understood that it was one of those inescapable things. He tried to plan for most contingencies he could control and gave it up to the gods if it was something he couldn't. For this particular run, he had a saddlebag full of herbs that he couldn't touch without gloves, and in the truck following him, his watchful cousin with a backseat full of potions. Will and Earl had made light the fact that they'd killed a Wulfen scout, but JT couldn't afford to ignore the ramifications.

The moment the crack of a gunshot sounded and his bike skidded, he understood that payment had come due. Distraction was partly to blame for him being taken unaware. His head had been filled with Nicole and their not-relationship. Luckily, his animal had stayed focused on its surroundings. His wolf braced, power flooding his body as he flew off the machine. He slid across the hot pavement, cursing but grateful he'd worn his leathers. He pulled out his gun mid-slide and fired at the wolf racing up the shoulder of the highway. The animal howled, dropping to the ground. JT grunted and rolled over when the dirt stopped his momentum. He landed in a ditch, the wind knocked out of him. Gunshots sounded around him, and there was no time to figure out injuries. He gave his wolf head and ripped through his clothes in the form of his animal. He took off for the highway, leaping at a man aiming a gun at the truck. JT grabbed him by the neck and brought him down to the ground.

He ripped through his shoulder and shredded the male's stomach with his claws. He charged after the next man before the one on the ground took his last breath. Dante ducked around the truck door and fired behind him, joining the foray now that gunfire didn't have him pinned. JT navigated through the ambush, he and Dante a coordinated unit as their fathers had trained them. JT hissed as a bullet struck him, burning a path across his shoulder, sending him down to the pavement. Pain bloomed throughout his body, and he shifted back to human, cursing. There was one final gunshot before the highway went silent around them.

JT rolled over onto his back and cursed again. A shadow landed over him.

"Sorry about that, Cuz, he got away from me," Dante apologized.

JT nodded and struggled to stand. "I hope you shot his ass in the balls. They were packing silver."

Dante's eyes widened. "The headshot was too good for him."

"Help me into the truck. We have to get this shit out." JT hissed.

Dante did as he asked, helping him into the passenger side. He threw JT's bike into the back and left the rest of the bodies scattered across the deserted highway.

"Phone," JT panted.

Dante handed him his cellphone, and JT sent out text messages. Their doctor would meet him at his mother's, and someone would come and clean up the mess they'd left behind. His hands were shaking as he sent out the last text, and he fought to stay awake. He looked down at his shoulder and saw angry red welts forming, following the path of silver in his system. He was fucked if they didn't get it out soon. It was his last thought before he passed out.

He didn't know how much time had gone by between when he'd

passed out and when he woke up. However long, he felt better, and his arm was no longer on fire. He blinked the grogginess from his eyes, and his mother came into focus. She sighed in relief and put a hand on his forehead.

"Your fever is going down. That's good," she whispered.

"How long was I out?" He asked hoarsely.

Valerie pushed a straw against his lips. JT took grateful gulps of the water. She took the cup away and adjusted the pillows below his head. He took a look around and realized he was in his childhood bedroom. King magazine covers and posters littered his walls. He grunted and tried to sit up.

"Lay your ass down, Jeremiah. Doc said to give it another day." Valerie scolded.

"How long have I been down?" He asked again.

"Two days," she answered reluctantly.

He cursed and tried to sit up again. While the silver wasn't actively burning through his bloodstream, he could feel the remnants. His muscles protested his every move. He sighed in frustration and laid back down.

"Send Dante to me, ma."

Valerie sucked her teeth. "You don't order me, cub."

"Ma."

His mother stared him down before shaking her head. "Fine."

He smiled as she left the room. He felt around the bed for his phone and sucked his teeth when he couldn't find it. He had a feeling his mother was holding it hostage. He gave up looking and laid back down, closing his eyes. The next time he woke up was to Dante standing at the foot of his bed.

Dante tossed JT's phone onto the bed. "What up, Cuz?"

JT shuffled to sit back against the headboard. "What did you find out?"

"No one is claiming the bodies so far. I'm still looking, though," Dante answered.

"The stuff?"

Dante looked away. "They got the shipment from the truck."

JT growled and moved his feet to the side of the bed. Dante came around and held him back.

"Your shoulder is still hot. Give your body more time to get rid of that shit. We got it. I'll find them. In the meantime, Yara is on the way to the drop with a replacement," Dante assured him.

JT growled and laid back down. "Let me know as soon as you find something."

"I got you. Rest. By the time you're ready, we'll have their ass in your office," Dante promised.

"Bet."

They both turned towards the front of the house as they heard voices.

Dante grinned down at him. "You got company."

JT grunted.

He tracked the voices down the hall as they came towards his room. His wolf sat forward, tired but excited all the same. Even though he knew she was coming, her presence still packed a punch when she entered the room.

"I'll keep you posted," Dante said, lifting his eyebrows and leaving.

Nicole waited until he left the room before rushing around to the side of the bed. "Are you okay?"

"I'm good, Nic," he told her softly, forgoing his usual teasing. Her distress was easy to read.

She touched his shoulder. "I heard you were shot."

He shrugged, grimacing at the way the motion pulled the already sore muscles. "My wolf took care of me."

Her eyes went wide, and she sucked in a surprised breath. "It helps you heal?"

He nodded. "I imagine your cat does the same for you."

"Interesting." She cleared her throat. "That's a good thing, then."

His mother came into the room with a plate full of thinly sliced steak. It was just on the other side of raw, the meat still red and tender.

"You need to feed your wolf, Jeremiah," Valerie scolded.

Nicole hastily moved. "I'll make sure he eats, Miss Valerie."

His mother eyed her, and JT worried what she'd say. Surprisingly she handed the tray over to Nicole.

"Ain't no choice, baby. His wolf will do what needs to be done. But, make sure he doesn't leave that bed," Valerie ordered.

"Dang, mama, I'm not going nowhere." JT laughed.

"Yeah, right," Valerie murmured, walking out.

Nicole stared down at the plate, her nose scrunched up. A distraction was in order.

"You gon' feed me?" He waggled his eyebrows.

She snorted. "I should let one of these half-naked women from these posters do it."

Her mean ass.

He swallowed a chuckle, took the plate out of her hand, and set it on the bedside table. "Come here, Fouche." He pulled her down into the bed with him.

"It's Oliver," She grumbled, burying her nose in his neck. "You scared me for a second."

He kissed her neck, tightening his hold on her and soaking in her scent. "Part of the lifestyle, Fouche."

She pushed back from him. "Getting shot is part of this couriering you do? You need another job," she grumbled, grabbing the plate again. Her hands were shaking as she picked up the fork.

He grabbed her wrist. "I'm good, Nicole."

She nodded and held the fork to his mouth. He dropped his mouth open and let her feed him. His wolf damn near purred, rolling through JT's body, enjoying her care. He didn't know if it was her or the food, but he grew stronger the longer she sat next to him feeding him. By the time he finished, he felt more like himself. Nicole caressed the side of his face as he took the last bite.

She stood, "You're supposed to rest, so I'm going to go. I'll call and check on you later."

He wanted to protest her leaving, but since he was in his mother's house, he thought it would probably be a bad idea to invite her to take a nap with him.

"I'm straight, Fouche. I'll be good as new in no time."

She leaned down and kissed his forehead. "I'll see you later, then."

JT slid his jeans up his legs and stretched. His wolf had finished healing, and he'd had enough of his mother's hovering. Spotting his phone next to the bed, he went through his messages. His smile was all teeth when he spotted Dante's message. He was close to finding out who had sent someone to take their stash. His stomach grumbled, and he headed to his mother's kitchen.

Valerie was at the stove when he padded in. He peeked at what she was stirring.

"I'm not eating soup."

"Ain't nobody said it was for you," she snapped.

He grabbed her around the waist and planted a kiss on her cheek. "Grumpy ass. I'm fine, mama," he soothed.

She scoffed and pushed out of his arms. He laughed at her stubbornness and went to her fridge. He smiled at the half-empty pie pan of peach pie, just enough for him. He pulled it out and removed the cellophane, grabbing a fork. He posted his uninjured shoulder on the wall and watched his mother. She eyed him, and he swallowed his smile with that first bite of pie. She was working up to a lecture. He could damn near see the words tumbling through her mind.

"I know your job is dangerous, Jeremiah. I done sewed your father and uncles up more times than I can count," she started.

"I'm careful, mama," he said around his next bite.

"You know what they say about them Fouches."

"Mama," he warned.

She stopped stirring and settled her hands on her hips. "I'm just saying. Why would you want to go and add additional danger on top of what you already do?"

He sighed. "So you blaming Nic for someone being dumb enough to attack us?"

"I'm not saying she's the cause, per se..." Valerie grumbled and turned back to her soup. "Ain't a woman in that family can keep a man, whether he dies or leaves. I'm just saying be careful."

"I got it, mama."

She turned and stared at him. "But you gonna do whatever you want."

"I'm grown." He smiled to take the sting out of his words.

"Fine, ignore the vast knowledge of all my years on this Earth," she fussed.

"Didn't you just cuss Jus out for calling you old? Now you have vast knowledge and many years," he teased.

She popped a dish towel at him. "Get out of my house."

He leaned over and kissed her cheek. "I'll be careful, mama."

"Where you going?"

"I gotta handle some stuff."

She sighed and pulled him into a hug. "Be careful, my love."

"Swear, mama," he said softly, kissing the top of her head.

She stepped back. "Wash that dish before you leave this house."

JT laughed and did as she ordered.

Chapter Twenty

The smells got to her first. The freshly churned dirt, the moisture-laden air that amplified the fresh smell of the pines encircling the property, it all undermined Nic's stony façade. Had she been inside doing any of the numerous tasks she had in her inbox, it probably wouldn't have been so bad. But now, she was on her knees in her grandmother's garden, giving the plants the loving touch and energy they had to be missing now that Patsy was gone.

Her chest ached, and unshed tears burned the back of her throat as she imbued power into the soil. She'd weeded already and watered them. That had to be done before the sun currently heating her back had risen. The flowers were now perking up, their petals opening, relishing both the sun and her magic. She continued singing to them, smiling as they swayed with every note.

"You're good at that." Audrey's voice broke through the grief clawing at her chest.

Nicole kept her head down, swallowing down the sobs fighting to escape. She pulled her magic back slowly until the tips of her fingers tingled. She slid her hands from the dirt, wiped them on her pants, and took a deep, shuddering breath, finally giving her cousin atten-tion. Audrey was sitting on the front steps, a mug in her hand, her dark eyes seeing too much for Nic's comfort.

Nic cleared her throat. "Thank you. It took me a while. I had to really work on it."

"I don't have a knack for the natural stuff. Grandmother kept trying." Audrey shrugged.

Adding jealousy to the mire of grief and hurt did Nic no favors. She clenched her teeth and breathed in and out until she could corral the chaotic magic.

"You seem comfortable with the hoodoo part," Nic finally managed.

Audrey's eyes narrowed on her. "I basically grew up with it."

"Must be nice." Nic turned her attention to putting away her tools.

"What does that mean?"

"It means you got to be initiated by our grandmother. I had to hunt down a stranger to figure out what the fuck was happening with me." And there went the tears she'd been fighting all morning.

"That's not my fault, Nic."

"I'm not blaming you, Audrey. I'm just saying." Nic stopped working and stared at her cousin, deciding the truth was the less messy option. "I'm jealous."

"Jealous?" Audrey said incredulously. "You had a halfway decent childhood. What is there to be jealous of?"

Nic cursed the tears she couldn't seem to stop. She'd been thinking about her grandmother the entire time she'd worked in Patsy's garden. Touching her tools and plants had her in a state. Her chest tightened, and she closed her eyes. She opened them and blinked away the moisture blurring her vision.

"You got to spend time with her, learn from her. You and Ness know so many people in town, and I just...I feel like an outsider," She finally whispered.

Audrey sighed. "Why didn't you come back?"

Nic shrugged and went back to weeding. "It was easier."

"Aunt Lauren can't be your excuse for everything," Audrey chided.

She sighed. "Your mother and Auntie Dawn, they used alcohol and drugs to push down on their power, I didn't..." she shook her head. "I felt like if I turned my head for one second, that it could be my mother. So I did everything I could to make sure that didn't happen. If all it took was for me to stay away from here for my mother to be stable, then that's what I would do."

Audrey's eyes filled. "That's a lot of responsibility, Nic," she whispered.

"No more than having to go into bars and pull your mother out," Nic said sadly.

Audrey stood and went to her, pulling her into her arms. They hugged long.

"Fuck, we're messed up, huh?" she said, wiping her face.

"Your mentor lives close?"

Nic shook her head, happy for the change of conversation. "South Carolina."

"I wonder if Auntie Shelby will take over for Grandmother. She's pretty powerful. She keeps the wards up over the property."

Nic frowned, "what wards?"

"You mean to tell me you don't feel them when we cross the property line?"

"I do, I just...damn, I can't believe I missed that. Do you think she'll continue teaching us?"

"According to Grandmother, the stuff I do is play-play. She was supposed to show me how to tap into our real power."

Nic froze. "Real power? You mean to tell me all this shit I can barely control is not our full power?"

Audrey snickered. "Trust me, I understand."

"Have you seen her yet?" Nic asked.

Audrey shook her head. "Not yet."

It was small of her, but Nic sighed in relief. One less thing she was being left out of.

"It would be great if she could come to us and say, 'this person murdered me.'" She shook her head.

"I know, right." Audrey sipped out of her cup. "Any more ideas about how to find the person who did it?"

Nic stood from her kneeling position and went and sat next to Audrey. "Ness is following the money, and other than studying the pictures Cellus gave me, I don't know what to do."

"Ok, well, changing the subject, have you given JT the jar?"

Nic groaned, "Can we change the subject to something else. What about some kind of sports ball? Who's playing in the Superbowl?"

Audrey snorted.

"Yesterday scared the shit out of me," she admitted to her cousin.

Besides JT getting hurt, it was the fact that it had taken two days for word to get to her. She had a feeling if she were Ness or Audrey, someone would've told her sooner. It made the sting of being an outsider worse. If it weren't for Ness talking to JT's mother, she probably wouldn't have found out at all. Thinking of him brought her to one of the reasons she was out in the garden early in the morning.

The more she was around JT, the more the puma that lived inside her body asserted itself. It had always been a part of the Fouche curse. None of the women had control of the cat, hence the many ways they'd chosen to cope with the feral animal. But lately...Nicole didn't want to say that she was bonding with the creature because she wasn't but, her magic was starting to meld with the power of the animal. Especially around JT. It was as though his wolf brought her animal out of the hibernation it went into the majority of each month. She battled with the cat only a few days before and after the full moon.

But here, home, the animal was starting to be more insistent. Is that why her mother had warned her to stay away? Is it why Lauren never set foot in Georgia up until the day of her mother's funeral? It would make a lot more sense. She needed to talk to her cousins about it. A part of her wanted to explore it a little more. Ness said that JT's family had trained her. Could they do the same for her? JT's wolf healed him; did their cat do the same for them? Now that she planned to stay in Georgia, she could look into it. She was done running from her family's legacy.

"I don't think the curse cares whether we like or love them." Audrey stood up, breaking into Nic's thoughts.

"So, not only were we cursed to shift into a cat we can't control, but we also get the bonus of losing the men we love." Nic sighed.

"Not just men," Audrey whispered.

"You were in a serious relationship with a woman?" Nic didn't realize her cousin was bisexual.

"Non-binary. They nearly died at least twice while we dated." Audrey shook away the memories.

"Is that why you came early?" Nic asked, remembering Audrey's vague answer at the time.

Audrey shook her head. "No, that was years ago."

"You're being evasive," Nic squinted at her.

"I got into some shit and need to lay low. Springbrook is as good a place as any to hide for a while," Audrey admitted.

Nicole gasped. "Is there anything I can do to help? Are you in danger?"

Audrey studied her before shaking her head. "Danger, no." She stood up. "Come on. I want to talk JT, anyway. Two birds and all that."

Nic blinked at the quick subject change but stood and followed Audrey into the house. She wanted to ask her cousin more questions, demand answers, but instead, possessiveness she'd never felt with anyone before rose up.

"What do you need to see JT about?"

"I need some stuff," Audrey said vaguely.

Nic growled at yet another non-answer. It seemed she wasn't the only cousin with trust issues. She couldn't be mad, though. They were nowhere near as close as they used to be when they were kids—something else she would need to work on.

"Let me shower then," Nic muttered, rushing upstairs.

Chapter Twenty-One

An hour later, Nic was pulling into the gravel lot of Lore. Motorcycles and men scattered the parking lot. Nic spotted JT leaning against a bike similar to the one they'd ridden on the other day. He had on black jeans molded to his thighs and a leather vest over his sleeveless shirt. His corded arms were out, covered in muscles and tattoos. Her breathing stalled.

"God almighty," Audrey whispered.

"Ain't he fine as hell," Nic said, resigned. No way could she resist this man.

As she drove closer and parked, she saw that a group of similarly dressed men surrounded JT. An older man stood next to him that had to be his father. JT looked like a younger, slightly darker clone of the handsome man. All eyes turned to them as they got out of the car. JT's hot gaze traced over her, and Nic prayed she wouldn't embarrass herself. She was happy to see him up and clearly over his injuries. She clutched the jar to her chest. She felt JT's gaze like a caress. Her body loosened and started to throb. Honestly, the effect he had on her body was different than anything she'd ever felt.

In comparison to JT's lust-filled look, the man next to him smiled at them both, his face relaxed, amused even though she could sense his wariness. He held out his arms as Audrey got closer.

"If it ain't Lil' Mama. How you doing?" The man asked.

Audrey laughed and hugged him tightly. "You can't call me that anymore Mr. Taylor. My mama looks after herself now."

Mr. Taylor's smile widened, warmed more if that were possible. "That's good to hear. She sober now?"

"Ten years," Audrey said, beaming.

Mr. Taylor kissed her forehead. "You gon' always be Lil' Mama, though. Sorry, thems the rules."

JT chuckled. "Pops, this is Nicole, Nic, my father, Will."

Nic held out a hand. Will eyed her and shook her hand. Her power flared a little as it met the heat of his. Age hadn't dimmed JT's father power one whit.

"I can't even fault you, son." His father said, his gaze raking Nic's face, his wolf lighting his eyes.

He was assessing her, which... was fair. Despite being familiar with her cousins, Will knew nothing about her. Some degree of scrutiny was to be expected.

"Can I talk to you for a second?" Nicole asked JT quietly.

He led her around the back and leaned against a gleaming black vintage pickup truck.

She was nervous about giving him the jar. It felt like such a big step to her. She didn't share her magic with anyone, not the people she encountered in her line of work, and not even boyfriends she'd dated over the years. Though 'dating' was a generous term for the relationships she'd breezed through. Either way, magic was so personal and intimate to her. Though her Aunt Shelby had done the bulk of it, it felt strange pulling JT into her life in this way.

She searched around for a stall tactic. "Why does your dad call Audrey, Lil mama?"

JT smiled. "She used to come through here to get her mother when Ms. Kit had had too much to drink. My mother calls her Mother Hen. Poor Audrey did a lot of mothering to Ms. Kit."

Her heart clenched, and she thought of the conversation they had just had this morning. Her cousin was so strong. JT tipped her chin up and dropped a light kiss to her lips, effectively pushing everything else from her mind.

"What you need, Fouche?"

She thrust the jar into his hands. "My Aunt Shelby and I made you a protection jar. I don't want anything else to happen to you."

A crooked smile was his answer. He took the jar, "where you want me to put it?"

"Anywhere in your house where no one will tamper with it."

"Done," he said, his eyes tracing her face. He wasn't scoffing or even looking skeptical. He took the jar and tucked it under his arms.

She cleared her throat, "how are you feeling?"

"Good as new, Fouche," he used his free hand to pull her between his open legs. He leaned his head over her neck and shoulders.

She shuddered as longing pervaded her body. JT scraped his teeth down her skin, sucking it into his mouth. His tongue licked across her skin, and she discovered something new about herself and what she liked. Because with every lap of his tongue and scrape of his teeth, her panties dampened.

"You miss me?"

"It's been a day," she said, suppressing a moan.

"Question still stands." He lifted her chin with his finger.

She stared into his dark eyes and nodded. He smiled and leaned down to kiss her. She eagerly opened her mouth, and their tongues dueled. She relaxed in his hold, his presence soothing the riot of emotions she'd experienced in her grandmother's garden. She wrapped her arms around his shoulders, her hand stroking the back of his head. JT pulled back and nuzzled into her neck again, sighing as she ran her nails down his neck. Nic closed her eyes and held him tight.

He lifted and nipped her lips, his smile warming her.

"I didn't even miss you a little," she lied.

He chuckled and bit her bottom lip again. "You and that cat. Mean asses."

He devoured her mouth once more.

JT made no moves to do anything more, just reveled in kissing her. He savored everything about her, her taste, the sensual little moans she made, all of it. His phone buzzed at his hip. He ignored it, for the time being, drawing out the kiss longer. When he was satisfied he'd gotten his fill, he backed up, pleased with the drunk look on her face.

"My job is dangerous, Fouche. You can't expect this jar to keep me out of everything," he warned her.

She sighed. "Noted."

"I got some stuff to do, now. But, what you doing later?"

"Nothing."

"Let's go out."

She nodded.

He intertwined their fingers and led her back to her car. Audrey was there chatting with his father. She stepped forward when she saw them.

"I wanted to ask you for some supplies," her voice was cautious.

He nodded and pulled Nic back into his body. He rested his chin on her shoulder, the need to touch her overriding everything else. "What you need?"

Audrey looked relieved. "I need gooter dust to start."

He had plenty of that. "That's easy enough. What else?"

She pulled a list from her back pocket and passed it to him. "I can pay you."

"You know better than that, Audrey," he murmured, skimming the list. His eyebrows raised at some of them. "I'll get what you need and bring it over."

She looked relieved. "Thank you, JT."

He slid the list into his pocket. "I got you."

He spun his stubborn mate around. He frowned at that term. His wolf had been pushing him since they'd first laid eyes on Nicole. Mate though? He'd have to consider that a little more in-depth.

"See you tonight?"

Nic tiptoed and kissed him, nodding. She pulled from his arms and headed back to her car. He stood next to his father, and they watched them go. Will whistled next to him.

"Your wolf likes to live dangerously," his father murmured. "I can't fault the animal. She's gorgeous."

And funny. And prickly. And so damn responsive. JT shook that last thought from his head. He had business to take care of, and thinking of fucking Nic to sleep was not part of it. At least not until later.

"I know you feel the strength of that cat she got hidden in there," Will said.

JT nodded. "I got it under control, Pop."

"Jeremiah, that one there is stronger than Ness, hell, she might even beat out Shelby and Patsy with the right amount of training. You need to move carefully, hear?"

"I hear you." He turned to his father and pulled him into a one-arm hug, balancing the jar in the other. "I gotta ride, Pop."

Will eyed the jar. "You taking that with you?"

"Nah. I'm taking it upstairs first."

"Be careful, son," his father told him.

"Always, Pop."

JT rushed up the stairs and set the jar on his bedside table. He smiled down at it because, whether or not she admitted it, he was getting under Nic's skin. His wolf was of a mind to rush the process, demand what he saw as his due, but the man understood the woman they'd chosen. He'd have to be sly to get her where they wanted her. The buzz of the phone in his pocket reminded him that he had places to be.

Chapter Twenty-Two

JT's wolf filled his body with excitement. Whether it be from Nicole's visit or the pending ass-whooping he planned on dishing out, he didn't know. He pressed down on the gas on his handlebar, and his bike sped down the near-empty street. He thought about the dents and scratches that had been on his baby from the accident and got mad all over again. It had cost him a pretty penny to fix it while he'd been down. For that alone, someone was going to pay. He carefully maneuvered his bike through the thick pines of the woods where he was headed until he reached a clearing.

Dante leaned nonchalantly against a tree; his tatted arms crossed over his chest. He had a male on his knees next to him, bloodied, his wrists tied in front of him. JT got off the motorcycle and lifted his eyebrows at the man's identity.

"Dang, Ced, I thought you knew better than to hit us on a run," JT said as he approached them.

Cedric shrugged, not scared or worried. "It's nothing personal, Taylor, just business."

Dante growled in irritation.

"I don't know, man, that silver felt real personal. What was the job?" JT crossed his arms over his chest and studied Ced.

The man stared at JT, and JT could see him weighing whether or not he'd be able to get out of the current predicament.

"The game is the game, JT. Someone paid me to hit you. We took the job."

"Hit me, or hit the shipment?" That was the more important question to him.

Ced shrugged again. "Just you. The package was a bonus. Made a pretty penny from it, too."

JT growled, his wolf riled. He could understand the hit; people came after them all the time. It was the supplies that pissed him off. It tainted his supply chain and confused his customers into thinking there were other options for their needs.

"See, that's where you messed up." JT drew a line in the sand with the toe of his boot. "This is your business." JT drew another line next to it. "This mine." He pointed. "See, they might be parallel, but ain't no reason for them to cross, you feel me?"

Ced looked nervous now. He looked around again, probably weighing his escape chances.

"Who ordered the hit?"

"I don't know. For real, JT. You know loners get hired all the time."

"You ain't just any loner, though, Ced. You know better than to fuck with Taylor wolves." Dante snapped.

"It won't happen again," Ced promised.

"It absolutely won't," JT agreed. He planned to make sure of it. "Who ordered the hit?" He asked again.

Ced swallowed. "I don't know."

JT pulled a gun from the holster on his back and shot Ced in the knee. The wolf went down screaming.

"See Ced, no silver bullets. Professional courtesy and all that." JT stepped down on the wound in his knee.

Ced screamed again, scrambling from beneath JT's boot. "I don't know shit, JT. I just took the job!"

JT's wolf filled his body, demanding to come out and finish the man himself. "Who ordered it?"

"I don't know!"

JT shot Ced's foot this time. "If you don't know shit, ain't no reason to keep you alive, then."

"No, no, wait," Ced panted, his skin ashen in pain. He held up his bound hands. "I don't know the name. It happened when I was hanging out in Savannah. The whole thing was anonymous," he rushed the words out.

"Where in Savannah?"

"I was in Poole gambling. Someone left the money and instructions on my bike while I was inside."

JT looked at Dante, and his cousin nodded, pulling out his phone. Leaning closer to Ced, JT snarled, his canines showing. He let his claws down, and his wolf howled in victory. He swiped the ropes around Ced's wrists to free him. Ced blew out a relieved breath that turned into a gasp as JT kicked him in the chest and into the murky marsh behind him.

JT watched dispassionately as Ced struggled to stand in the muddy water. "The game is the game, Ced. If you manage to leave my territory alive, I'll consider it a lesson learned."

Ced fought to come ashore.

JT shot the ground in front of him. "Aht-Aht. Can't come back this way."

The male growled but struggled to swim towards the other end of the bank, dragging his injured leg behind him. It was a manageable distance to the other side. Taylor land covered a large area full of all manner of predators, though, so Ced had his work cut out for him. Especially if he continued in the direction he was swimming. His Uncle Nathan didn't like surprise visitors.

"He'll wash up," Dante warned JT coming to stand next to him.

"Good," JT murmured. "We like a strong message."

Dante snorted. "We got a couple of contacts in Poole. I'll see what I can find out."

JT nodded and handed Dante the gun. His cousin slid it into a bag he pulled out his back pocket. He would get rid of it in case Ced's wolf didn't push out the bullet in his knee before his body was found.

"Let me know what you find out," JT murmured.

"Where you headed?"

"I got a date to plan," JT told him, getting onto his motorcycle.

Dante smirked. "A date, huh?"

"I'm a gentleman."

"My ass," Dante laughed.

JT walked to his bike. "I'll see you later."

Dante gave him a salute before shifting and loping off into the woods. Ced's chances of leaving the woods alive just decreased by half. JT shook his head and cranked his bike, dismissing the situation. He had plans to seduce the mean Ms. Oliver tonight, and nothing would get in the way of that.

Chapter Twenty-Three

The images in front of Nicole were starting to go fuzzy around the edges as she continued to stare. Nothing about them had changed in the days that she'd been studying them, but all the same, she turned the paper slightly.

No change.

She sighed and dropped the picture back into the pile. Lifting the whole file, she figured coffee would help. Audrey was already in the kitchen fixing herself something to eat.

"Are you just now eating lunch?" Nic asked, dropping the pictures onto the counter.

Audrey nodded and peered at the folder. "What's that?"

"Cellus got images of the crime scene as the police found it," she told her, starting the coffee machine.

Audrey spread the pictures across the counter. "Is she…"

"No, no body. Just all the damage. I can't imagine how Aunt Audrey felt coming back in to clean up."

"Uncle Brandon did it," Audrey said off-handed as she perused the pictures.

Leaning against the counter, Nic frowned. "I didn't know that."

"He and Aunt Becca did." Audrey ate her sandwich, going through the images.

They both turned towards the back door as someone knocked. Nic smiled as she spied Cellus through the glass.

"Cellus, hey! I was going to call you later," Nic pulled him into a hug.

"I needed to clear my head, so I came to check on you guys," He said, walking in and dropping a kiss to the top of Audrey's head.

"We're making it," Nic told him.

Cellus took a look around the kitchen, his face tightening. Nic didn't need her magic to sense his grief.

"I haven't been here since...."

Nic nodded, understanding. "We were just talking about what a great job Uncle Brandon did cleaning the place."

Marcellus walked the length of the kitchen and peered into the living room. "He even changed some stuff around."

"What do you mean?" Nic walked over to him, trying to see the room with new eyes.

"They rearranged the furniture looks like," Marcellus murmured.

"Which furniture?" Nic's gut started churning, something telling her that bit of information was significant.

Cellus walked back into the kitchen and picked through the pictures. He plucked one from the lot and held it up. "See, the sofa and stuff are moved around."

Nic took the picture and studied it, comparing it to the current room. She noticed the bookshelves had been moved as well. She frowned because a painting had been there in its place.

"What happened to this artwork?" Audrey asked, staring at the picture over Nic's shoulder.

They both turned to Cellus.

"I don't know. Maybe they took it. Brina painted it, and Uncle Brandon is always encouraging her." Marcellus frowned.

"Shit, your ten-year-old painted this?" Nic said incredulously.

"She's good," Cellus murmured, heading to the bookshelf that was covering where the painting would've been. "Help me move this."

They carefully shoved the bookshelf to the side, and she gasped at the sight of the safe. She and Cellus shared a look.

"Oh my God! Grandmother was hiding a safe in the wall?" Audrey rushed over and peered over their shoulder. "Anyone have the combination?"

Nic wracked her mind for where that information could be. Maybe her grandmother's journals, the lawyer's paperwork? "I have a few places I can look."

Cellus put his hands on top of his head. "What in the world? Why wouldn't Uncle Brandon tell us about this?" He pulled his cell phone out of his pocket.

She and Audrey shared a look and shrugged.

"Ma. Did you know Grandmother had a safe in the living room?"

They couldn't hear the other end of the conversation. Cellus sighed. "Yeah, we just found it. Do you know what the combination could be?" He paused. "Oh, ok. I'll call you back then. Love you."

"What's going on?" Ness walked into the living room. "ooh, a fire-guard safe. Nice!"

Nic and Audrey turned to her.

"How in the world do you know that?" Nic asked.

"I know stuff." Ness shrugged.

"Can you open it?" Audrey asked, narrowing her eyes at her.

Ness squinted. "It's hella old." She walked over to it and put her hands on the safe. "It's got an old Sargent and Greenleaf lock. I could probably open it with a little time."

"What is it that you do for a living, Vanessa?" Audrey folded her arms over her chest.

"I mind my business. You?" Ness tossed back.

"So, is that a yes or no?" Cellus cut in to stop their potential bickering.

Ness raked her eyes over them all before nodding. "Yeah, I can get in. Let me go see what Grandmother has in the garage."

"What do you think is in there?" Nic asked when Ness left.

Cellus shrugged. "Probably old family papers?"

"Money?" Audrey said. "Maybe what the robber was looking for?"

"There was no damn robber," Nic muttered.

They turned as Ness came back with an electric drill.

"You're gonna drill a hole in it?" Cellus asked, frowning.

"Nah, I'm going to fiddle around with the dial a bit and listen to the tumblers to see if any land. Last resort is the drill." Ness explained.

"Listen to the tumblers?" Nic frowned. "With what?"

"I know you girls don't fuck with the cat we have under our skin, but the Taylors have taught me a thing or two about using the instincts that come with this curse," Ness murmured, leaning her ear against the safe.

She and Audrey shared a skeptical look and turned back to Ness. It confirmed everything she had been thinking about bonding with her cat. If Ness could use the animal, surely Nic could be taught to as well. She made a mental note to ask JT the next time they talked.

"Now, no more talking. Let me see what I can do."

"Got it," Ness announced an hour later.

"Thank God!" Audrey declared, sitting up from where she was lying on the sofa.

Nic shook Cellus' shoulder where he'd fallen asleep. "She got in."

Cellus wiped his face. "Word?"

They all stood behind Ness as she opened the safe. Nic held her breath, anxious and curious in equal measure.

Audrey sucked her teeth. "No money."

Ness snorted but then gasped. "Look at all these pictures!"

Nic took the fragile pictures from her as she handed them back. She passed them to Cellus, reaching for the old book Ness passed next. Walking from them, she carefully opened the leather-bound book.

"Oh shit," she whispered.

"What is it?" Cellus asked.

"Great Grandmother's journal," she breathed out, awed to have the history in her hand.

"Wow, that's amazing," Cellus murmured, studying it over her shoulder. "You'll have to show mama. She would love that."

Nic nodded absently, wanting desperately to dive into the pages now.

"Bingo," Ness announced.

Nic whipped back to her. "What did you find?"

"Remember the lawyer said Grandmother had an audit done, but he never got the results?" Ness held up a folder with the audit company's name on the top.

"Open it," Audrey rushed her.

They all gathered around Ness as she did. They passed the pages around as Ness pulled them out of the envelope.

"Get to the final report," Nic said, equally impatient.

Ness nodded and shuffled the pages until she came to the end. Her eyes skimmed over the words quickly. "Someone was stealing from the company."

They all looked up with various looks of surprise.

"Not someone. There can't be that many people with access to be able to do that," Nic pointed out.

"Fuck," Cellus whispered.

"This doesn't mean anything," Ness said.

"It's a motive, Ness," Audrey corrected.

"Who has access?" Nic asked, running through the information through her mind. Their...Uncle...she looked up at Cellus.

He shook his head. "I don't believe he'd do something like this."

His voice was pleading, and she understood he'd never want to think that a family member had done it.

"Well, we have all the financials. Let's go over it first before we start accusing people," Audrey said hastily.

"Murder is a big leap from theft," Ness said.

"That's fair," Nic admitted. Not like she wanted to accuse her family of anything.

"So, we agree. We investigate this a little more before we go to Uncle Brandon?" Cellus asked.

They all nodded. She was sure none of them wanted to be the one to do it either way.

Chapter Twenty-Four

He wanted to play it cool. That was the intention when he'd gotten dressed this evening. The whole way over to her house, JT had coached himself and his wolf. Nicole was not a woman for keeps. She'd made that clear every time they slept together, and he was okay with that. Problem was…his wolf had other plans. Even now, the animal had him revved, the thought of her sending a cacophony of emotions through his body. He'd readily agreed with her that their relationship would be easy, no strings attached. That was how he viewed all his relationships, so why was this so hard? Was it the magic of the Fouche women?

He shook his head and knocked on the door, breathing deep as he waited. This wasn't high school. He was grown, damn it. The mix of panic and excitement should not have him double-checking his outfit. Still, he brushed a hand over his pants. He stood taller as the door opened.

Attraction was one thing. The way his breath stalled when he saw her was a whole other thing. JT tamped down on his wolf as it bucked, his muscles clenching with the effort. Her scent traveled to him, and he damn near called the whole thing off. He wanted her.

He shook his head because that was too tame for the molten need that filled him. It burned away all the walls he kept up around his heart and mind. That had never happened before.

Nicole smiled at him as she stepped closer, the dress she wore swishing around her thighs. It had a deep vee in the front that gave him a mouthwatering view of her cleavage. He grabbed her hand and spun her, enjoying the way her dress flared and swirled her. He pulled her into his arms.

"You look amazing," he whispered as he nuzzled into her neck.

"Thank you." She kissed his cheek and stepped back.

He looked up, and her cousins were staring at him, their eyebrows lifted. He cleared his throat.

"I'll be out all night," Nic told them as she grabbed her purse.

JT helped her into her jacket.

Ness snickered before heading back to whatever she'd been doing before she answered the door. "Don't do nothing I wouldn't."

"Well, that means nothing's off the table," Audrey muttered, turning her attention back to the television.

"Good night," JT called out as he herded Nic down the steps of the porch.

"Don't mind them," Nic said.

JT guided her to his truck, his eyes tracing the long expanse of leg. Helping her into his truck, he leaned over as Nic settled into the seat. He slid a hand up her thigh. She stopped him before he got too far.

"Aht-aht, you're taking me to dinner," she admonished, kissing his lips lightly.

He chuckled and deepened the kiss. It would be a miracle if he made it through a whole dinner. "I'll behave."

Though their conversation was light, the tension was thick in the air between them as he drove over to one of the islands off the coast of Westport. He'd made a reservation at one of the finer restaurants there. He wanted to impress her. By the time they were seated at their table, JT had to chug the water there waiting. Nic smiled at him before burying her head in the menu. He needed to get his hormones under control. He perused the menu. He was calm by the time the waiter was back for their order.

He looked up once he was done ordering and found her watching him. "What?"

"You look handsome," she commented.

He adjusted the slacks he wore and popped the collar on his tailored shirt. "I clean up well."

"Yes, yes you do." She licked her lips.

"Didn't you tell me to behave," he said low, his wolf filling his voice.

She sighed and sipped from her wine. "Right, sorry. Let's talk."

That worked for him.

"How do you like living in such a small town?"

"I love my family, I love this land, and I can't imagine living anywhere else." He answered truthfully. He was more than content with his life and lifestyle.

She looked around. "Are there a lot of shifters here?"

"This town used to be a refuge for all kinds of supernaturals. We could hide here easily, and the local government knew not to bother us. That was over a hundred years ago. There are fewer types of shifters here now that we no longer have to hide from humans."

Her eyes widened. "I didn't know that." She frowned. "Actually, Jesus, why didn't I know that?"

He laughed at her puzzled face. "I take it you were a quiet kid?"

"According to my cousins, I was sheltered," she grimaced.

"I believe it. Ness said you travel for work. You don't run into shifters on your job?"

She shrugged. "I have, but this town is different. I feel like it's wilder here. There's a kind of magic in the air that I've never experienced before."

"Could be because you're connected to this town. Even with supernaturals being public with their existence, we're still wary of strangers." He told her.

She smiled, liking the thought of that.

They got quiet as the waiter placed their food on the table.

"You've asked about my work. What is it that you do? I only know vague details from your cousins."

"I work for FEMA. I work in the southwest region. I get called to whatever disaster site is in my area, take assessments and determine what it will take to get the place back up to some level of normal." She answered.

"Is it hard?"

She shrugged. "I really like it. Not the disasters, but being able to offer help."

"So once you are done settling Ms. Patsy's affairs, then you'll be back on the road?" He asked carefully.

She paused with her fork at her mouth. "You know, I'm tired of the impermanence I've been living with. I'm making plans with my supervisor to work from here. I'm ready to settle down."

She finished her bite, and then her eyes widened. She seemed to realize what she said because she choked and took a deep swig of her wine.

"Not that I'm hinting or anything or like, rushing through this, I'm just—" Nic rushed out.

"Take a breath." He grabbed her free hand and fought to keep the amusement off his face.

She blew out a breath. "Sorry."

He smiled. "So you're ready to settle. Do you like it enough to settle here?"

She took another deep sip of her wine. "When I got the paperwork that Grandmother had left us everything, it felt like a sign, know what I mean?"

He nodded. "Ms. Patsy did a lot of work on the property."

She nodded. "I love it. I think, though, that eventually, I'll want my own place. It's a little big for me."

"Fouches got property all around there, though, right?" He resumed eating.

"Yeah, my mother has her own plot. I think I want to build there. It's right by that lake Grandmother had dug eons ago." She also went back to eating.

"Talk to me about that cat of yours," he said softly.

She looked up like a deer caught in the headlights. "What about it?"

"It's powerful, but I can tell you're having a hard time controlling the power that surrounds it." He thought back to their sex, and the wild way her cat interacted with his wolf.

She shrugged. "I don't control it at all, to be honest. I just try to keep the magic from getting out of control on most days."

This time he frowned. "My dad taught Ness how to control it somewhat. Haven't you had anyone to do that for you? What about your mother?"

"My mother ran far and fast from her cat. She suppresses it as much as she can, and when she can't, shifting is this big secret she keeps to herself every full moon." Nic sighed.

He reached out and grabbed her hand. "I hate that for you. I can't imagine not being bonded with my wolf."

"So tell me about you, is the bar the only place you own?" She took her hand back and resumed eating.

He shook his head, allowing the subject to change. "I have a few places scattered from here to Jacksonville. A bar, some warehouses, them mini shopping centers. Trying to flip the money so that by the time my sister and cousins finish college, they'll have something legal to run."

She smiled, pleased with his answer. He ignored the pride that gave him.

"Your sister's in college now?"

"Yeah, she got a couple more years left."

"Y'all close?"

He smiled and nodded at the thought of his wild-ass little sister. She was a wolf through and through. And though he worked to make something legal for her, she was a Taylor, so he knew it was only a matter of time before she was hustling. He and Dante had tried to keep Yara and Justine on the straight and narrow, but so far, they were keeping Jus in college by the skin of their teeth.

"I like that." She said with another sweet smile. "I wish I had siblings."

Dinner passed with more conversation between them. He liked that they were able to talk. He paid for dinner and guided her back to his truck. They were quiet on the way back to his place. He probably should've asked if she preferred him to take her back home, but he wanted more time with her. The heat between them pressed against him, tension tightening his stomach. Her cat's power pressed against him, nearly taunting his wolf. From their conversation in the restaurant, it was something she couldn't control. That feral magic wrapped around him, its alluring heat causing his hands to shake on the steering wheel. He pulled around the back of the club and went around to open the door for Nic.

She wrapped her arms around his neck as he lifted her from the truck. Nic leaned down and kissed him, opening her legs to cradle his body between them. He groaned and deepened the kiss. He skimmed the soft skin of her thighs and groaned as she shivered. Anticipation had his hands shaking.

"Inside, now, Fouche," he whispered against her lips.

He wrapped her legs around his waist and walked her up the back stairs to his apartment. They were barely through the front door when she impatiently unsnapped the buttons of his shirt. She pushed it off his shoulders, not relinquishing his mouth. He walked them through the apartment, laying her gently on the bed. He followed her down, putting his weight on her body. He guided her arms above her head, slowly rubbing himself against her body. She squirmed beneath him, dropping kisses along every part of his body she could reach.

She tightened her legs around his waist, lifting her hips in invitation.

"Relax," he whispered, rubbing his face down her arms.

He nibbled at her ears, grinding his erection into her. She sighed in languid pleasure. Using one hand, he pulled down the straps of her dress, using his teeth to pull down the bodice.

"Keep your hands up," he ordered.

She nodded eagerly. JT kissed a line across her chest as he pushed the rest of his shirt off. He unzipped his pants, and she used her feet to push them down around his knees. Free of their clothes, they connected, and he entered her smoothly. She was already wet and ready for him. JT worked his way back up to her mouth, kissing her softly, his tongue teasing hers. She sighed at his gentle caress. He spun her around until she was on her stomach, her arms still extended.

He kissed along her shoulders before entering her. Her body stretched to fit him, and she moaned as he filled her, each push better than the last. She turned her head, and he leaned down to kiss her. She hungrily tangled her tongue with his. She pushed her ass up, and he pulled her tighter into him. Pressure built up, heat overtaking his body.

Their pace increased until finally, they both climaxed.

JT relished in her warmth, snuggling into her back. He would want her again before the night ended, but he needed just a moment to rest...

Chapter Twenty-Five

Even before he opened his eyes, JT knew the space next to him would be empty. The ephemeral Nicole had once again disappeared before the sun could rise. Any other time, he'd be happy. No awkward conversation, no reiterating the lack of permanence in their relationship. None of that needed to take place with Nicole. But, he was feeling some type of way about her insistence that she couldn't stay even one night with him.

Despite all signs to the contrary, JT still felt the bed next to him. He sighed at the cool sheets. Her scent lingered where her body heat didn't, and that seemed all the more torturous. Groaning, JT rolled from the bed and headed towards the shower. The sooner he removed her scent from his space, the sooner he could function without obsessive thoughts of her. He turned around and stripped the sheets from the bed for good measure, dumping them into his hamper. He snapped the leash on his wolf tighter. They would not spend all day with Nicole on their mind.

His phone was ringing when he stepped out of the shower.

"Yeah?"

"We need to ride, Cuz, got a lead." Dante's voice was gruff.

"Give me five."

He hurriedly dressed, sliding weapons into place in case it turned into that type of trip. Dante was downstairs waiting on him in his muscle car when he reached the bottom step. JT jumped in, and off they went.

"Where are we going?"

"Poole. I talked to Jermaine. He said Dom wanted to talk directly to you," Dante answered, merging onto I-95.

JT grunted and fondled his telephone, debating sending a text to Nicole to let her know he was leaving town, however temporary. He swallowed a sigh because doing it wasn't conducive to keeping up his carefree lifestyle. He would have never done it with anyone else, and that was telling. It was a two-hour drive to their destination, and he spent most of that overthinking the direction he and Nicole were going.

Dante pulled up to the warehouse district, and they looked around before getting out. JT fondled the knife at his waist and slightly let his wolf off the leash. His senses cranked up, and he scouted the area. Operations were in full swing when they arrived at the door. The shifter guarding it gave them a look but moved to the side.

"He's waiting for you in the back," the man said gruffly.

JT nodded, and he and Dante made their way through the illegal make-shift casino. The tables were full, a low throb of desperation and buzz of excitement filling the space. Dante covered his back as they went down a dim hallway. JT knocked on the office door and was let in by a massive bear shifter.

"Taylor!"

The dark skin man stood up, his nearly seven feet making the bear at the door look small in comparison. It was expected of the Alpha to be bigger than the rest, and Dom exuded that, as well as a dangerous aura that said size was not the only thing he brought to the table. JT's wolf sat forward, tense, ready for trouble.

"Dom, how's it going?" JT nodded to the man's enforcers behind the desk.

Dom sat back down, settling his bulky body into the oversized leather chair behind his desk. "I wanted to see for myself that you were still on this side of the veil."

"I ain't easy to kill," JT said dryly, sitting in the chair in front of him. "What you got for me?"

"I got word Dante was asking around about Ced's movements, so I decided to check it out myself." Dom swung his computer monitor around.

JT leaned closer to see the black and white surveillance video. He narrowed his eyes as Dom clicked the mouse and the high-definition video played. They all watched a shifter he didn't recognize stop next to Ced's bike and slide a package into his storage compartment.

"You know him?" JT asked, sitting back.

Dom shook his head. "Never seen him around here. I just wanted you to know that I had nothing to do with the attempted hit on you."

"I'm glad to hear that, Dom. We have a great working relationship. I would hate to have that fucked up."

"Same," Dom commented.

"You could've emailed this. Why the meeting?" JT studied his longtime associate.

Dom sighed and sat forward. "From what I've been able to gather, it's one of the northern wolves."

JT frowned. "Wulfen?"

"I don't want to start a war on my end with misinformation, but that's what it looks like," Dom said with a shrug.

JT's wolf filled his body, his anger rising. He shared a look with Dante. He was already typing, hunting for more information.

"I'll keep your name out of it, of course," JT murmured, standing.

"I got your back regardless of what you find out. I ain't scared of them little shits."

JT chuckled.

"From the information I'm getting, the Wulfen have a new alpha, and he ain't in control of the wolves."

JT frowned. "What does that mean?"

Dom shuffled uncomfortably in the chair. "From what I can tell, they're under the control of a practitioner."

JT and Dante shared a look. There was only one practitioner powerful enough to control a whole wolf pack. If it was Jedidiah, then Dom wanting to speak to him personally made more sense. Jed could make work uncomfortable for Dom if he wanted to.

"Jed called me looking for supplies. You think he'd order a hit on me?" JT asked.

Dom shrugged. "Everything I know is from other sources. The shifter could be from someplace else. Maybe the Wulfen have nothing to do with it. Either way, I wanted to look you in your eyes and tell you that me and mine don't have any hand in it." Dom came around the desk and held out his fist.

They bumped knuckles, and Dom walked him back out through the door. JT paused as he reached the end of the hallway and squinted as he recognized one of the players at the poker table. It wasn't that he was surprised to see humans mingling in a mostly shifter area. He was just surprised by which human it was.

"She come here a lot?" JT asked.

Dom followed his gaze and chuckled. "She got herself a gambling problem. She owed me a pretty penny a while ago, but she paid it off last month. I haven't seen her in a while. I guess she's back, flush with cash."

JT flicked his gaze back to her and filed that bit of information away. If she was coming all the way to Savannah to do her gambling, that probably meant she'd been banned at the spots in Westport or hiding. It could be either. He wondered if Nicole knew what her aunt was up to. He turned back to Dom.

"As always, Dom. Appreciate you," JT dapped him up, and he and Dante left.

Dante saved his questions until they hit the highway. "What do you think?"

"I think the Wulfen are getting bold, unnaturally so. A new Alpha doesn't give you that level of bold."

Dante surprised gaze flickered over him before going back to the road. "So you think Jed has control over them?"

"Yeah, the math ain't adding up," JT murmured, going through all the events that had been happening lately.

"What should we do?"

"Let me think on it some more." JT looked out at the passing trees, his wolf restless. He looked to the sky and realized why. "Full moon run tonight?"

"Hell yeah," Dante agreed.

With the pack at his back and cold night air blowing through his fur, JT was at his happiest. It was one of the main reasons he never wanted to leave his hometown. Here, he had the freedom to run and shift and the space to do so. The dampness of the air around the marsh called to him and his wolf. His pack answered his howl as they ran through the woods. His wolf was single-minded in its destination and purpose. He jumped over a fallen tree and hastened his steps as the midnight moon filled the sky.

His wolf was excited, and inside the wolf, JT was aware that the animal was headed for its mate. He stopped at the property line, a wave of power flowing over the pack. They all skidded to a stop behind him on instinct. He knew Ms. Patsy kept a ward over her family's land, but his wolf had ignored that human warning. JT tossed his head back and howled, calling to his mate. His wolf took another step forward, and the heat that usually blasted him when he reached that line in his animal form was missing. He pawed the ground and took another step closer. His wolves went to follow and couldn't, surprise spreading through the pack link.

He looked back at them and made eye contact with Dante, and the wolf threw his head up and down in acknowledgment. He would keep the pack there to wait on JT. When he turned back towards the Fouche house, he saw three large pumas waiting. They were twice the size of a wild Puma, the only thing that distinguished them as shifters. JT howled again, and they came closer. He could pick out Nic, not sure how he was able to, but he did, his wolf responding to her by rubbing their coats together. He nudged them towards the wolves and the property line. Ness took off, used to running with the pack. The other two were more hesitant, but eventually, they went.

He led them through the town, avoiding the street, giving their cat the leeway to run and hunt with them. He knew from his father that the cats would do so regardless, but they would be safer with the pack. They ran through the night, his wolf and Nicole's cat sticking close together, the cat even nudging him, testing his strength. He could feel the moon's power waning signaling early morning. He howled and sent his wolves on their way, guiding the Fouches back to their property. He felt when they crossed the power line and could still go through—an intriguing development.

He guided the women up to the front porch and shifted. He went inside and grabbed blankets, spreading them over each cat. He waited patiently through their shift, talking their pumas down from taking off. The animals only reluctantly ceded to his wolf after some growls and nudges from JT.

He winced as they came out of their shift one by one. Their bones were popping, and it sounded painful. Ness was first, her cat used to relinquishing control. He knew from experience that she would be out of it. JT bundled Ness' sleeping form in the blanket she was under and carried her inside, taking her to the room that smelled the most like her. He did the same for Nic and Audrey, waiting out their cat's stubbornness. Once he carried them all to their rooms, he shifted to his wolf and inspected the property for intruders, and made note of a couple of spots where there were foreign scents. He would check them tomorrow. He ran back to the house, shifting as he jumped onto the porch.

He turned around as headlights pierced the darkness. He cocked his head and inhaled, relaxing when he realized who it was.

Dante stepped from the pickup truck, a bag in his hand. "I figured you wouldn't want to be far from your phone."

"Good looking out," he murmured. He didn't bother getting dressed.

Dante waved and went back to his truck. JT waited until he'd driven off before entering Patsy's house. He locked the doors and took a shower, settling behind Nicole, very content with their run together. He knew she didn't like her cat, but his wolf was very happy with the beautiful animal. He fell asleep, cuddled into her.

Chapter Twenty Six

Nic woke up the following morning, her body sore as hell as it always was when they shifted with the full moon. She hated it, hated that part of the curse more than anything. She just prayed she didn't do anything the night before. It slowly dawned on her that she wasn't outside in the dewy morning grass. That was the first thing she noticed. The second was poking into her lower back hard and insistent.

She whipped around, shocked to find JT staring at her. She started to open her mouth to ask him what had happened, but then she tasted the copper tang she associated with blood and immediately rushed from the bed. She'd barely made it to the toilet before she threw up. *Oh God, what the fuck happened last night?* What was the blood she tasted, animal or human?! She threw up again.

"Animal," JT's morning roughened voice answered.

Her head lifted, and relief like none other flooded her body. She rested her forehead on the toilet seat. Oh, Thank God. Wait...how had he known what she was thinking? She stared at him with widened eyes.

"Trained Ness, remember?"

"Oh, yeah." She sighed and stood, going to the sink and washing her face.

She grabbed an extra toothbrush and passed it to JT. He took it, and they brushed their teeth in silence. Was it awkward silence? Sometimes she couldn't tell. She studied him.

"What happened?"

It frustrated her to no end that she never kept any memories of her shifts. It was scary to wake up the next day and not know what happened for the six or so hours her puma took control.

He spitted into the sink, put the toothbrush down, and headed for the shower, naked as the day he was born. Her eyes widened and dropped down to the morning wood he was sporting. He gave her a cocky smile that made her want to drop to her knees. He winked and started the shower.

"My pack took you running," he finally answered.

"You came and got me?" She forced her eyes up to his face.

"Y'all," he answered.

"All three of us?" Now she was even more confused.

He walked over to her and lifted the shirt she wore. That was when it became apparent she wore no underwear.

"You saw us all naked," she accused.

He chuckled and got into the shower stall. "Get in the water, Fouche," he ordered.

She stepped into the hot water after him.

He pulled her into his chest, nuzzling her neck. "Good morning."

"You saw my cousins naked." She repeated.

"Does it help to know I only responded to one naked body?" he murmured against her neck.

That actually mollified her. Still... "Audrey's gonna freak."

"I was very respectful, Nicole. Would you rather I have left the three of you in the front yard?"

Her shoulders relaxed because that had happened more times than she cared to admit. Of course, not her grandmother's yard, but she'd woken up in the bushes of many parks. She had no control over when she changed into the cat or back to human.

"No, of course not. Thank you."

"You're welcome, darling. Now..." he hovered over her lips, their heated breath mingling. "Can I get my morning kiss or what?"

She went up on her toes, their first kiss soft, exploratory. He'd taken care of her last night, and she was a little scared with how much that softened her. She needed to remain strong, steadfast in their relationship being a brief fling. The more time she spent with him, though, the more he showed her the softer side of him...

She was fast losing the fight with her feelings. JT gripped her chin to deepen their kiss until she was panting. His erection was poking into her stomach, insistent. The urge to take care of him was overwhelming. She pulled back from their kiss and soaped up a washcloth. She bathed him, the bathroom silent, neither of them breaking the spell they were under. She gently pushed him into the water lifting his feet one at a time to lather them and rinse them off. She was at his waist when his erection nudged against her shoulder. She looked up at him, a soft smile tilting her lips, and kissed the bottom of his shaft softly. He leaned back into the shower wall, a groan tearing from his throat. She traced the water down his chest, stomach, and hips, with her free hand, letting it run along her lips as she slid up towards his throbbing head.

She sucked the underside of the tip of his head and used the washcloth to open his thighs, gently cleaning and tugging his balls. He groaned in response to the sensation. She teased the tip of his head with her tongue, gazing at the stream of water flowing along his body. He stretched, trying to push into her mouth, and she moved aside, gliding her lips along his shaft again. Cloth tossed behind her. She wrapped both hands around his shaft to control his movements.

She worked back towards his head, pulling his hardness into her mouth squeezing him as she slowly sucked him into her mouth. He held her head, urging her lower. His head knocked against the wall, his body jerking when he touched the back of her throat. His breath was ragged with need as he guided her speed.

"You can take all of me," he coaxed her, his hand spanning her neck.

Nic shivered as flames of desire licked across her skin. Her sex fluttered, need for him spurring her to take him deeper. JT growled and gently pulled her to her feet, scooping her into his arms.

"My God, that mouth of yours," was his heated whisper as he savagely claimed her mouth.

Their tongues dueled as he walked them back into her room. They left a line of water behind them, and she hastily grabbed towels from the rack as he crossed the threshold of the bathroom. She tossed them down on the bed a moment before he did the same to her.

"Legs open, Fouche," he ordered.

She complied immediately and hissed in pleasure as he roughly pushed into her. He grabbed her legs and wrapped them around his waist as he buried himself inside her causing her breath to hitch. He leaned over, nuzzling into her neck, pulling her skin into his mouth as he drove deep, stretching her inner walls around him. Her eyes closed, her power rose, their animals rising as energy and heat built between them. Their hips moved together, both of them desperately clinging to each other.

She grabbed his head, pulling him close, pushing her hips higher to take him deeper. She needed to feel him closer.

"Harder," she whispered, desperate.

She wanted to consume him. Her power melded with his, intensifying his every stroke. Frantic and scorching magic washed through her body and flared out to fill the room. JT groaned, his fingers digging into her hips as she bucked beneath him. Her eyes popped open as he hit that spot deep within her that had her careening toward a climax. His eyes were glowing with his wolf; his bottom lip clenched between his teeth. He was beautiful, and a possessive wave overcame her. He was hers. The cat inside her surged forward, and she gripped his head, bringing him into her neck. Yearning filled her chest, and her breathing stalled as JT skimmed his teeth down the column of her neck.

His wolf prodded against her psyche, and her cat answered back. She scraped her nails down his back, and he growled into her skin before biting down hard on her shoulder. A blinding orgasm powered through her, and she screamed. Relief, euphoria, and a heady sense of vindication filled her. Her cat damn near preened in her body. JT jerked once, twice before growling and pushing into her body a final time, a long moan signaling his orgasm. Her pussy clamped down hard, holding him, owning him.

His wolf's power raked across her skin, and her cat responded in force. They both jerked, a release plunging them in pleasure for a second time. Nic could do nothing but hold tight to JT as her body ignited. Their souls intertwined, and their power melded, flowing between the two of them in a blazing display.

It was long moments before their bodies relaxed, their caresses softer, the overwhelming power and need cooling. Nic stroked his back in lazy circles luxuriating in their closeness. She'd thought coming back to Georgia had felt like home, but this...this in JT's arms...there were no words.

He sighed and rolled over, bringing her onto his chest. She closed her eyes and settled on his chest, listening to the rapid beat of his heart. She wanted to relax, to enjoy this moment, but her body was thrumming, realization crashing down on top of her.

They were bonded.

JT pushed her wet hair to the side and kissed her forehead. "You realize we spent the night together, right?"

It was just a little joke. But it was compounded with the fact that they'd bonded themselves together. Nicole had fucked up, and now JT would pay the price for it.

Chapter Twenty-Seven

er panic was a suffocating blanket. His wolf whined, not understanding what was happening. JT pulled Nicole into his chest and held her tight. Her muscles were tense, despite what they'd just shared. He cursed internally for his slip up. How could he make that kind of mistake?

She pushed her hands against his chest. "I need…"

JT released her immediately, and she scrambled from the bed.

"Nic, it was a joke."

"Okay, but the bite on my shoulder is not," she murmured, grabbing clothes from her dresser drawer.

"I'm sorry, I lost it with my wolf," he admitted, the euphoria from that moment lost.

A tense silence descended, and JT scrambled to find some way to diffuse it. His phone rang from the pocket of his jeans. He ignored it, focusing his attention on the woman who didn't want to be his mate. It hurt, and his wolf was damn near inconsolable. The phone stopped ringing, and the silence that followed was somehow louder. Until it started again.

"You need to get that," she snapped, heading towards the bathroom.

He sighed and padded over to his phone. "Yeah."

"I'm texting you a list. Can you do it today?" It was Jedidiah.

JT studied the closed door between him and Nicole. She obviously needed space. "Yeah, I can do it. Be prepared to sign the contract." He warned him and ended the call.

He scanned the list Jedidiah sent before forwarding it over to Yara. She was closest to their stash house. He dialed Dante next.

"Cuz. It's early as hell," Dante complained.

"We gotta do this run to Jedidiah."

"You want to run four hours out of the blue?" Dante's voice was suspicious.

JT touched the bathroom door. It may as well have been a solid steel wall. The sounds of the shower and fan running filtered through, and through their new bond, he could feel her turmoil. He fucked up...bad. He wished he could say that he regretted. He'd gotten caught up in the moment. Her power had been heady. Even now, he could feel the undercurrents of it roiling through his body. His wolf had fed from it, giving her some of theirs in return. The exchange of it had taken his breath away.

He'd fucked up.

He sighed. "We got something else today?"

"No, I'm not saying that. Just making sure you want to do this now."

He turned his back to the door. "I want to see if he has control over the Wulfen. If not, then we can sign the contract, and he'll be one less problem for us to deal with."

Dante was quiet for a few moments. "What happened?"

"Te, I can't get into it now." His heart clenched, and he fisted his hand at his side.

He could still feel the wet slick of her skin beneath the pad of his fingers and the ghostly clasp of her sheath. She was an addiction.

More so now that they'd bonded. He growled and slid his pants up his damp legs. He wouldn't be in the pants long anyway.

"You want me to come get you? You still at Nicole's?" Dante was wary.

"I'll shift and meet you at the clubhouse." JT ended the call and turned back to the bathroom door.

It opened, and Nic gasped and stepped back. They stared at each other, neither of them saying anything.

JT closed the gap between them and lifted her chin. "I'm going on a run. I'll probably be gone until tomorrow."

She nodded. "Be careful," she said softly.

"We got a lot to talk about, Nic." It wasn't what he wanted to say at all.

"I need a minute, JT. Please?"

That would have to be enough for now. She wasn't outright rejecting him, but somehow his wolf was not getting that message. The animal clawed within him, despondent at the tumultuous feelings within her. He studied her eyes, searching for...what he didn't know. He knew she worried about the effect the curse would have on him. How in the world would he get past her reluctance? It was a problem for later, especially seeing the stubborn set of her mouth.

He sighed, kissed her forehead, and left her room before he pushed. He waited until he was into the woods before he stripped and let his wolf loose. The animal howled forlornly, but JT exerted his will over his wolf and pushed him towards home. They couldn't go back. At least not until the both of them calmed down.

Nicole dropped her head the second she heard his howl. It was pain-filled and full of the same confusion tightening her shoulders. She trailed her fingertips across the healing bite JT had left on her shoulder, and a lump gathered in her throat. What had they done? If they were lucky, this ride they were on wouldn't end in his death. Perhaps they'd escape only hating each other like her parents. A scream built in her chest, and she wished she could release it the way his wolf did. But, the full moon had passed, and though her cat was anxious inside of her, exerting its presence, it wouldn't come out until the next one. The Fouches couldn't shift at will like a regular shifter. Never before had she wished for that freedom.

She swiped the tears from her face and finished getting dressed. She needed to get out of this room. She was happy the kitchen was empty when she walked in minutes later. She started breakfast. She was whipping the eggs like they'd personally called her names. She growled when Ness rounded the corner, cutting into her pouting time.

"What's wrong with you?"

"Nothing," she snapped and turned towards the stove.

"Well, them eggs won't be fit to eat after you're done slamming them around in that bowl," Ness said nonchalantly.

Nicole said nothing, but she did stop beating the eggs. She went into the pantry for bread.

"Ugh, it's tense in here," Audrey said as she came in.

"You can always leave," Nic muttered.

"Unh-unh, I can't deal with a stank attitude this early in the morning." But Audrey didn't leave; instead, grabbing the bacon from the refrigerator.

"This definitely calls for liquor," Ness said, pulling out sparkling wine.

"Lord, not this early in the morning," Audrey told her, pulling out aluminum foil.

Ness shrugged. "I'll make mimosas, and then it will be respectable."

Audrey snorted and studied Nic, but said nothing as she prepared the air fryer. Nicole didn't fill in the silence; instead, she dunked the bread and made French toast. Ness passed her a glass of mimosa and sat down at the table.

Nic set her glass down hard after she downed the contents. "I don't want to talk about it."

"You the only one talking," Ness said, taking a dainty sip out of her glass.

"It could help you to get it out, though, if you're taking suggestions," Audrey said in a prim voice, sliding bacon onto the air fryer trays.

Nicole poured herself another mimosa, this one heavier on the wine. She narrowed her eyes at her cousin. "It's none of your business."

Vanessa snorted.

"When did you get so damn mean?" Audrey asked, chugging her drink and fixing another. "You were never this mean when we were younger."

"You don't know me like that, Audrey. I've always been like this," Nic snapped.

"We grew up together. I do know you," Audrey defended.

"You knew me as a kid, that's it." Nic threw back another drink. She growled because the mimosas weren't going to get the job done. She needed to hunt down a more potent liquor. "The last time we spent more than an hour together, we were what, eight?"

"Ten," Audrey said softly, "dad died picking me up from the airport."

"Oh, shit. I'm sorry, Audrey." Nic felt like shit.

"Yeah, you sorry." Ness threw back her drink, no longer bothering with sipping, "sorry as hell."

Nic sighed and leaned her head forward, arms on the counter. "I'm sorry, that wasn't fair, and I shouldn't be taking my anger out on you guys."

Ness fixed another drink. "What you mad about?"

"JT probably," Audrey muttered. "Although I can't figure out why. The two of you been banging on the walls in your room for hours, so I don't understand the problem."

Nic clenched her jaw around the words. Yes, she'd grown up with her cousins, and yes, they fell right back into their pattern when they'd arrived, but she'd never been one to share. Still, if anyone understood her dilemma, it would be them. She flopped down on the dining room chair.

"I like him. Like, really like him." She yanked at the collar of her shirt. "And he did this, this morning."

Ness and Audrey leaned over to get a look at the bite.

"Well shit," Ness whispered and threw back another drink.

"Nothing positive?" Nic turned towards Audrey.

Her cousin's eyes watered, and she took back another drink. "What the hell can I say? I've lived that curse first hand," she whispered and turned back to her cooking bacon.

Nicole reached across the table and touched her cousin's back.

"We should try and break it," Ness said.

They turned to her in shock.

"How?" Nicole tried to keep the desperation out of her voice, but it was there, along with hope.

"Aunt Shelby said they stopped trying," Audrey said.

"The three of us are barely initiated. How in the world can we do it?" Nic asked, her shoulders drooping.

They were silent, each of them digesting the size of the problem. They all jumped at the knock at the back door. Marcellus walked in a file folder under his arm.

Nic wiped her face and stood to get back to breakfast. "You want some French toast, Cellus?"

"I could eat," He said carefully, his gaze bouncing between the three of them. "What did I miss?"

"Nothing for you to worry about," Ness said, standing and refilling the pitcher.

"What you got?" Audrey asked, following him to the table.

"I think I'm ready to question Uncle Brandon," Marcellus announced.

"Chile," Ness whispered, shaking her head.

"That's right, we still got a murder to solve," Audrey said aghast, dropping her head to the table with a bang.

"It's too much going on," Ness said, sitting back down.

Nic cooked and said nothing. What could she say? She'd let JT distract her from the reason she'd come back to Georgia in the first place. Now, instead of figuring out who killed her grandmother, she was worried about breaking a centuries-old curse so that she could be with him. Lord, have mercy. She sighed and slid the finished toast on a platter.

"Did you find anything differently on your end, Ness?" Marcellus asked to break the tense silence.

"Everything I saw matched what the auditor found. The financial stuff the lawyer gave us didn't match the financial information that Grandmother had given the auditor." Ness answered.

Nic put the platter on the table. "Which means she didn't tell the lawyer."

"That's why he didn't tell us," Audrey said. "Dang, can you wait on the bacon?"

"You're welcomed to eat whenever the hell you'd like, Audrey," Nic said sweetly.

"So damn mean," Ness muttered into her glass.

"A simple yes or no would've sufficed," Audrey said, rolling her eyes.

Cellus laughed and fixed his plate.

Chapter Twenty-Eight

JT was happy he'd let Dante drive up. His head was everywhere but the task at hand. Wrestling his wolf back into human form for the ride north had been bad enough. The closer he got to Jedidiah territory, the more anxious the animal got. It wanted to be closer to Nicole, and every mile they put between them, the harder it was for him to wrangle the wolf. Bonding with her had been a bad idea. Besides the fact that she wasn't ready, now his wolf would pine for her until she was.

He wiped a hand down his face and forced his mind back to the upcoming meeting. Jedidiah would probably still want to fight with him regarding signing the agreement, but he would be ready. He didn't foresee doing any business with the rootworker without some guarantee in place. Jedidiah was power-hungry, and JT didn't want his wolves to become fodder for whatever Jedidiah did to gain that power. Dante slowed the truck down as they left the highway.

"You ready?"

JT nodded. "I have to protect our wolves; otherwise, you know how he is."

"We can just not do business with him. There's money to be had elsewhere," Dante cautioned.

"Yeah, but Jed controls the territory all along Northern Georgia. If we don't deal with him, that cuts down who else we can deal with up this way." JT murmured.

Dante sighed and pulled into the long dirt driveway that would lead to Jedidiah's house. Trees surrounded the road on both sides, and the truck shook as they rode over the pockmarked driveway. Dante pulled into the yard, and they stared at the rootworker's house. There was nothing to mark it as anything other than the country house it purported to be. Except the hair raised on his arms and his wolf paced his body as the power and magic that saturated the land seeped into him.

Dante turned his head to him. "Cuz?"

"I know, Dante. But this will get him off our back. I don't want unnecessary enemies." JT reached behind him for the duffel that carried Jedidah's supplies.

Dante nodded, but JT could feel his cousin's wolf. It was just as anxious as his. He calmed the animal and walked to the door. He rang the doorbell and waited, scenting the air.

JT frowned. "Something's off," he said softly.

"I feel it." Dante touched the gun at his side.

Jedidiah answered the door in a cardigan and chinos, looking like a retired doctor. The white of his beard and hair contrasted with the cocoa tone of his lined face.

"Jeremiah Taylor."

"Jedidiah," JT greeted.

Jedidiah stepped to the side to allow them entrance. JT and Dante both waited until the rootworker preceded them. He was a man they didn't want at their back. JT had never been inside Jed's house, so his eyes raked the area, taking in everything from the books scattered haphazardly everywhere to other escape routes.

"Would you like something to drink?"

JT shook his head and plopped his duffel bag on the kitchen counter. "I don't have all day. You want supplies from me; then I'll get your signature."

Jedidiah smirked, and JT's wolf sat forward, nervous energy flooding his body. The protection tattoos along his back warmed. JT pulled the contract out of his bag. Ms. Patsy had given him a lot of them, the spells on them binding and infused with magic JT hadn't bothered trying to decipher. He'd gone to another rootworker to double-check this one for Jedidiah in particular. He didn't want the rootworker going back on his word.

The smirk dropped from Jedidiah's face, and greed filled its place. "Where did you get magic this powerful?"

"I got friends, Jedidiah. I don't know why you think I would fuck with you without them." JT shook his head and slid the parchment over.

Jedidiah turned, suddenly stalling. "A blood contract is very solemn."

"You talked all that shit. I'm here; let's do this," JT said impatiently.

Jedidiah cleared his throat. "I can't enter into a contract with you."

JT didn't say anything despite the anger blazing through him. He rolled the contract up and tucked it back into his bag. "Let's roll, Dante."

"Wait. I can give you something else." Jed reached out his hands to stop them.

"Your money don't mean shit." JT headed for the door, pissed.

Dante pulled out a gun and pointed it at him as he turned.

JT stayed calm, at least on the outside. Inside, his wolf was shredding at the cage keeping him tethered. He wanted out.

"What you doing, Cuz?"

Dante's hands shook. "I can't control it, JT."

JT let his wolf off his leash, leaking out his alpha power. That power reached for his cousin but was blocked access. He eyed Jed, who had a smug smile on his face.

"I think we can deal now," Jed said lowly.

JT reached into his bag and put the contract back on the table.

Jedidiah's smile spread wider. "I'm not signing that."

He grunted and reached deeper into his bag and pulled out a powder he'd had made for such emergencies. He took it and blew it into Dante's face quickly before Jed could try and stop him. His cousin blinked and pulled the trigger, but the shot went over JT's head, an involuntary flex of his fingers. Dante shook his head, and the powder settled, his eyes clearing. He turned the gun to Jedidiah.

The rootworker put his hands up and hastily spit out, "I took another contract on you."

"The fuck you say?" JT stepped closer.

Jed was nervous at first. And then the house shook. Jedidiah's hands moved, and JT cursed as something grabbed from behind. The stench of freshly turned earth and death choked him as a creature he knew could only be a ghast lifted him from the ground. Jed was known for turning the shifters he'd killed into them to do his bidding. JT half-shifted and raised his claws, raking at the undead's arms. He growled when nothing happened. It wouldn't release him. He turned forward, using the momentum to toss the monster over his head as he slid through its grasping arms.

The monster crashed at Jed's feet, making him stumble back. The undead ghast immediately shook its body, rolling back to its feet and charging for JT again. Cursing, he shifted, giving control over to his wolf. Dante lifted his arm to shoot again when a wolf flew from the living room, crashing into him, sending him into the kitchen table. JT knew his cousin would be fine, so he focused on the bigger problem in the room.

The ghast reached for JT, but he darted to the side, biting into the undead's calf. He wanted to gag at the rancid taste; instead, he bore down until he reached the bone. The creature didn't balk at JT's attack, merely grabbing him by the fur and lifting him from the ground. He flailed as the creature seized his throat, struggling to get in air. The stench filled his nostrils, and the lack of air had him seeing stars.

Just as the edges of his vision went black, Dante crashed into the ghast's back, raking it with his claws. It threw the monster off balance, slamming it and JT into the wall. JT used that opportunity to swipe at its face, taking out one of its eyes. The creature howled, his grip loosening. The shifter Dante had been fighting threw itself onto Dante's back, and the two of them went at it.

"Kill him!" Jed yelled.

They nipped and clawed each other looking for soft spots. Anger had JT seeing red, and as though summoned, the power he'd gotten from Nicole during their bonding swelled in his body. The tattoos along his back heated, and strength flooded him. He shifted back to human, leaving his claws. He needed to end the ghast before the fight got any worst. The creatures were notoriously hard to battle, and he'd heard many stories about them. JT rolled to the side as the ghast lunged at him, kicking at the back of the monster's knees.

He needed to get back to his bag. He gave a hasty look around the kitchen and spied the leather duffle against the wall. He slid near it and was just reaching inside when the creature grabbed the back of his neck, slinging him across the room. JT growled, pissed, but nowhere near as hurt as he should've been. He didn't have time to examine why. He pulled the stopper from the bottle he'd managed to retrieve, slinging it at the advancing monster.

Jed screeched in anger, and power swelled in the room. "Finish him." He hissed.

The monster was stumbling, the potion JT had thrown onto him, finally working its magic. He wanted to breathe a sigh of relief, but he wasn't quite done yet. The monster head-butted him, and JT fell back. Dante kicked aside the shifter he'd killed and picked up the sawed-off shotgun that JT carried in his bag and fired into the ghast's skull. He racked another bullet into the chamber and pointed it at Jed.

The old man started chanting, feeding power into his creature, but it was no use. Parts of the monster were already disintegrating under the spell JT had thrown onto him, Dante's shot to its head speeding along the process. JT rolled over, groaning in pain.

"Take him out, Te," he wheezed, fighting to get to his feet.

Jed threw magic towards Dante, sending him and the gun slamming through the wall and into the next room. JT dived for Jed while his attention was averted. He shifted his claws at the last minute, raking them across the practitioner's neck.

"I warned you," JT growled, breathing hard as Jed slid to the ground.

The old man held his neck, his blood sluggishly leaving his body. The practitioner was murmuring, using his other hand to reach into his pocket. JT beat him to it, ripping the vial from Jed's hand.

"Will this help save you?" JT taunted.

Jed closed his eyes, and the wounds on his neck started knitting themselves together. JT barely stopped himself from flinching at the sound of a gunshot. The practitioner's body jerked, and blood bloomed along his shirt. JT looked back and breathed a sigh of relief as Dante limped into the room.

"Next one goes into your head." Dante coughed.

JT turned his attention back to Jed. "Who did you have the contract with?"

Jedidiah shook his head. "Leave my property now while you have the chance."

JT raised his head as he heard the howls of wolves coming from a distance. He pushed his foot into the gunshot wound on the practitioner's shoulder. Jedidiah shouted out.

"Who?"

Jed didn't answer, instead raising his hand. Dante's next shot hit the rootworker's other shoulder, and Jed collapsed onto the tile.

"Once you're dead, the wolves you've been imprisoning will be free. Do you imagine they'll still do your bidding?" JT whispered, leaning into the wound.

"I want the Fouche land," Jedidiah wheezed. "You were in my way."

"The Fouches would never give up that land." JT looked up as the howls got closer. They had moments before whatever other shifter Jedidiah had called to come to his rescue burst through the doors.

"I had a blood contract...." Jedidiah struggled to breathe as he bled out on his once pristine tile. "Rebecca Fouche...I bought out her debt...she would turn over the land."

"Fuck!" JT hissed.

His wolf desperately clawed at his chest. They needed to get to their mate. JT grabbed the gun from Dante and killed Jedidiah, having no need for any other conversation. JT searched the kitchen for his phone, hoping it was in one piece. He sighed in relief and dialed Nic's phone. It kept ringing until the voicemail clicked on. He slammed a hand against the wall in frustration. He hastily threw on the spare clothes he kept in the duffel, throwing a pair of pants and shirt to Dante.

JT searched the house until he found Jedidiah's office, turning it over and dialing Nicole while he searched. He finally found what he was looking for in an open lockbox in the desk drawer.

"Dante, let's roll!"

"Right behind you, JT," Dante rushed around the corner. "I took care of the body."

"The gun is clean, right? We'll ditch it on the way home," JT said, racing for the door.

They slid as they reached the truck and found it surrounded by wolves. He didn't have time for this shit.

"Move, I'm only going to tell you once," JT snapped.

The young wolf held his hands up and backed away from the truck. "It was you who took care of Jedidiah?"

JT nodded, fast walking to the truck, but his eyes never left the wolves.

"We owe you a debt," The young wolf spoke.

"Jeremiah Taylor. Look me up in a few days, and we'll handle that."

"And we'll take care of things here," the male said.

JT nodded, and he and Dante got into the truck and peeled out. He hoped he made it to Nic in time. With Jedidiah dead, he didn't know what desperate thing her aunt would do to cover up her crime.

Chapter Twenty-Nine

Nic sighed as JT called her phone again. She declined the call and, this time, shut her phone off. She didn't want to deal with him at the moment. He'd bitten her, bonded them, and now turbulent feelings twisted her insides. It would be so much easier if she could blame it all on him. But her cat, that stupid animal she had no control over, had reveled in his bite, pushing her power to meld with him. If she were being fair, she could admit that she'd done nothing to stop it. But panic was leaving no room for fair.

Fuck, she felt closer to him, like he was under her skin, his wolf's power warming her from the inside. The hardest part of it all was that she'd craved it. She'd damn near pushed her shoulder beneath his teeth and begged for it. God, what was she going to do? She didn't want to end up like the rest of the women in her family.

The Fouche curse had not missed a single one of them, and she was next. Her breath hitched, and she looked out the window at the passing trees. They were headed to the Brewery to confront their uncle for stealing money from their grandmother. Why wasn't that enough to keep her mind off of JT? Probably because she could feel him inside of her anxious, or was that anxiety coming off her? She didn't know anymore. She shuddered as she remembered the feel of his teeth on her shoulder. For a few minutes before the panic, there had been absolute bliss. It was as though a weight had been lifted from her chest. That feeling of closeness had filled every empty spot inside her heart and soul.

And then reality crashed down.

Even now, hours later, she wanted to hyperventilate with the thought of losing him. And she would lose him. The curse hadn't missed yet.

"Nic," Ness said softly next to her. "You sure you don't want to sit this out?"

She shook her head and clutched the file folder to her chest. "I'm straight."

Her cousin eyed her. "I can feel your cat's power. It's damn near pushing mine forward."

Nic shrugged because there wasn't anything she could do about it at the moment. She'd been trying to wrangle the magic down for the last hour. Something had it agitated. She looked down at the phone and wondered if she should be checking in with JT. Could he already be in danger? Was the apprehension filling her body from the upcoming confrontation with their Uncle, or was it coming from JT's wolf? She knew nothing about bonding with a shifter and thus had no way of knowing.

Denial and impulsiveness had robbed her of proper preparation. She knew nothing about what to expect of the bond, which made their situation precarious. It added to her turmoil. She turned her phone in a circle, guilt prodding her to turn it on and answer his call. She shook her head.

Later.

She'd have that talk with him later.

Marcellus parked the car, and they got out, heading to Uncle Brandon's office. The Brewery was closed to visitors, and only a few of the staff remained. Nicole hoped they didn't make a scene. It was one thing for them to accuse their uncle of stealing. It was a whole other for the employees to hear that.

"We should've done this at home," she murmured.

"The records are here, though," Marcellus told her in a soft voice as they passed another employee.

She nodded and filed behind them as they headed to their uncle's office. Uncle Brandon was sitting behind his desk when they came in. He smiled for a moment before frowning.

"What's wrong?" Brandon took off his glasses and studied them as they came in.

They closed the door behind them, standing in front of his desk.

Nicole pulled the paperwork out of the folder she was holding and slid them onto his desk. "Grandmother had an auditor look at the books before she died."

Her uncle's face went slack, the blood draining as he slouched back in his office chair. He took a shuddering breath before covering his face with his hands.

"Uncle Brandon," Cellus whispered. "Tell me the numbers are a mistake."

Brandon moved his hands and took another deep breath. "They're not." He finally admitted in the tense silence.

Ness cursed, and Audrey gasped, turning away. Nic couldn't turn away. She wanted to know his every reaction, needed to understand.

"You were stealing from Grandmother." She didn't make it a question.

"I am responsible for what happened, yes," he admitted.

Nic frowned at his odd wording.

Audrey noticed it too and whipped around. "What does that mean? Why say it in that manner?"

"At the end of the day, it's my responsibility to ensure that the company is run right and above board," he answered.

Which...to her way of thinking was another non-answer.

"What does that mean?" Marcellus demanded, his hands slamming down on the desktop. He leaned over. "Are you also *responsible* for her death?"

Brandon stood and met Cellus' ire. "I would never hurt my mother! I don't care what you think about the stealing, but surely you wouldn't believe that of me."

"You knew Grandmother wouldn't call the police. How did you convince her to let you keep your job?" Audrey asked.

"Or didn't you? Was that why she gave us the brewery?" Nic asked, putting the pieces together.

Brandon flopped back down in his chair. "Mama confronted me about it after she received the audit. I volunteered to step down."

Nic frowned. "When did this happen?"

"Two days before she died," He admitted.

Cellus paced away from the desk, his face etched in pain.

"We know Grandmother wasn't killed in a robbery. Yours is the next strongest motive," Ness pointed out. Tears made her eyes luminous.

"I swear I didn't hurt my mother," Brandon insisted. "When I told you girls I would show you the ropes and retire, I meant it. I have no intentions of fighting to hold on to this company. After what I did…" He broke off.

Nic sighed and gathered the pages back into the folder. She didn't know what to believe. "How were the numbers right when the lawyer audited after grandmother's death?"

Brandon cleared his throat. "I put the money back."

The cousins all exchanged surprised looks.

"So you had eighty thousand dollars laying around? Why steal in the first place?" Ness asked hands on her hips.

"All you need to know is that it was taken care of, and now that you have inherited it, I won't be able to touch another dime." Brandon held up his hands.

"That's not good enough!" Cellus barked.

"It will have to be," their uncle said quietly.

"Where did you get the money?" Nic asked.

He turned his head and didn't answer. Which didn't bode well because what did he do to get that money? And more importantly, what consequences would it have?

"You've gotten all the answers you're getting from me," their uncle said stubbornly. "And, until you girls take over, there is work for me to do, so...you should leave."

"I'm not dropping this."

"This isn't the end."

Marcellus and Nic spoke at the same time. They turned and shared a look that was a promise to each other.

"Uncle Brandon," Audrey pleaded.

"No. I've said all I'm going to say on the matter. It was handled when mama was alive. There's no need to rehash it now." Brandon put his glasses back on and went back to whatever work he'd been doing on the computer.

"How can we trust you? For all we know, you could rob the company blind on your way out." Nic snapped.

Ness gasped and turned to her. "That's too far, Nic."

"He's the one hiding shit, but I'm taking it too far?" She threw her hands up in frustration.

"Either of you is welcome to start now, today. I can teach you everything you need to know to keep that from happening," Brandon said quietly.

He was hurt, and Nic felt like shit for the accusation. She was raw from her interaction with JT and wholly out of patience. She walked from the office, unable to take it.

She took a deep breath of the humid, cool air the moment she hit the sidewalk outside. She blinked back the sting of tears and paced, willing her body to give up the outward signs of its turmoil. What had she expected to find when she showed up to solve a murder? Her mother had warned her that she would shake up family secrets best laid to rest. She should've listened to both of her parents. Had she done that, she'd be on assignment someplace where no one knew her, happily blending into the background and staying out of the family drama. She certainly wouldn't have her heart poised on the edge of the tearing and rendering that the family curse would do to it.

Shit.

She leaned against the hood of Marcellus' car and lowered her head. What would she do about JT?

At the thought of him, she pulled her phone from her pocket, turning it on. Her stomach dipped in nervousness. It rang the moment it powered up. If it was him again...

She cursed. It was worse. "Good morning, mom."

"What's wrong?" Lauren asked.

"Why would anything be wrong?" she hedged.

Her mother sucked her teeth. "Nicole."

"Mom, I'm not in the right headspace to talk about it," she admitted. She looked up as her cousins came out of the brewery. "I have to go. I'll call you when I get back to Grandmother's."

She stuffed the phone into her back pocket and faced them. She frowned as she realized Audrey was missing.

Ness answered her unspoken question. "She's staying to 'learn the ropes'."

"Are you sure that's a good idea? He could be a killer." She turned to Marcellus.

He shrugged. "I just don't know, Nic."

"Uncle Brandon is not a killer," Ness insisted. "And trust me, Audrey can take care of herself."

Nic sighed and dropped it. "So he didn't say anything else?"

"Just kept denying he had anything to do with Grandmother's death." Marcellus kicked his front tire.

She put a hand on his back. "You don't really believe he'd have anything to do with it anyway."

"I know that, but he's hiding something, and that something could help find out who did it." Cellus jerked open his truck door.

Nicole sighed and jumped into the back seat. "What's our next move?" she asked when he and Ness settled into the front.

"We need to find out where that money came from," Ness

murmured, studying the building. "If it's a bank, then it is what it is, but eighty k that fast is fishy."

"Agreed," Nic said. "I also want to know who actually stole the money and what they did with it."

Marcellus turned to face her. "You don't think he did it?"

"He as good as admitted he didn't. Who would he cover for?" Ness asked them.

Her eyebrows raised. "Now, that....that's a great question."

Chapter Thirty

"You're avoiding me."

Nicole sighed and sat on the top step. "I'm not, mom."

"Lies," Lauren snapped. "I know you like to pretend you slid out of my vagina fully formed, Nicole, but you come from me. Are of me. You think I don't know when something is going on with you?"

Nicole covered her eyes and lowered her head. She'd managed to avoid the cussing out she knew was coming for hours. Night was falling around her, though, and Lauren was done waiting.

"Mom," she started.

"Why do we have to live like this, Nicole? Why won't you talk to me?" Lauren sounded tired and guilt prodded Nic.

"Because I'm not in the mood to argue with you if I'm being honest."

"We don't have to argue," her mom interjected.

"And yet, you didn't start the call with 'hello, Nicole, are you okay I was worried.' You started it being snippy," Nic reminded her.

Lauren groaned and ended the call without another word. Nic sighed and put her head down on her knees. It had been a long day.

She'd been avoiding both her mother and JT for hours, stalling both confrontations. She'd been helping Ness track down the money her Uncle had gotten to replace what had been stolen. Ness had some contacts that Nic was almost positive weren't legal, but she didn't want to look too deep. So far, they hadn't found anything, and when Audrey got home, she said Uncle Brandon hadn't told her anything more.

It was all a dead end.

Her phone rang again, this time with a video call. She shook her head and answered.

"Mom."

Lauren's eyes traced her face. "I've been anxious all day, Nicole. I can feel something wrong. Tell me what it is."

Nic shook her head. "It's stupid, mom."

"Is it anything to do with your Grandmother's death?"

Nic perused the background of her mother's video. Lauren was driving, her face made up, and diamonds sparkling from her ears. "Where are you going?"

"A fundraiser. I'm meeting Gerard there," Lauren waved her hand. "Back to the subject."

"Uncle Brandon or someone he's covering for was stealing from Grandmother's company," she told Lauren.

"What? Brandon? I don't believe it!" Lauren looked around. "Hold on. I have to pull over."

Nic's lips twitched in a small smile. Her mother said she wanted nothing to do with family drama, but she loved to gossip. "He admitted to it. But then he said he paid it back. Where do you think he could've gotten eighty thousand dollars?"

"Eighty thou—" Lauren took the phone off the holder. "Wait a damn minute. Mama had that much money in her little beer company? And Brandon stole it? Shelby must not know."

"I thought it could've been a motive for Grandmother's death, but he's insisting that he didn't have anything to do with it." Nic swiped away some bugs. "I don't know what to think."

"Your uncle does not have eighty grand sitting around. I can tell you that. Kit told me Becca spends money before it barely settles into their account." Lauren confided. "Well, did mama know he was stealing?"

"According to Uncle Brandon, she confronted him. But then after he promised to put it back, she dropped it."

Lauren scoffed. "Bull shit. Your Grandmother held grudges with all ten fingers and toes."

Nicole had to chuckle at that bit of truth. "That's what he said, and she didn't call the police, so...."

"Mama would never call the police; you know that. Maybe that's why she left everything to the three of you?" Lauren pursed her lips.

"That's what we were thinking." Nic sighed, tired of thinking about it. "What's the fundraiser for?" She changed the subject.

Her mother narrowed her eyes but allowed it. "The local library. Don't think I don't know what you're doing. What else is bothering you?"

"I met a man here," she confessed.

Lauren's eyebrows shot up high. "A man you're telling me about, that's new."

"He's different, mom." She didn't know what to say outside of that. She and her mom didn't have the type of relationship where they shared much with each other.

"You're worried about the curse?" Lauren gave her a sympathetic smile.

Nic shrugged.

"I've told you about living in fear of that curse, Nicole. You'll miss so much of your life trying to avoid it. Love is fun, exciting. Quit running from it." Lauren sounded wistful.

"He got hurt. It would be one thing if we just ended up like any of your other marriages, no offense. What if it ends up like Aunt Kit's or Auntie Shelby's?"

That was her genuine fear. She could maybe handle if they broke it off, never to see each other again, but to know she'd caused JT's death. She didn't think she could live with that.

"Oh, sweetheart." Lauren sighed. "You can't control every aspect of your life. Whatever happens, will happen with or without your input. What if while you're expecting the worst, the best thing that could ever happen to you passes you by?"

Nic chewed on that, nodding. She raised her head when she heard the sound of a truck coming down the street. Her heart started beating fast. Was it JT? Was she ready to talk to him?

"I gotta go, mom. I love you."

"Love you too, baby. I'll call you tomorrow," Lauren promised.

Or threatened.

It depended on how Nic felt tomorrow. Such was the relationship she had with her mother. Though, now that she thought about it, she wanted to change that. She'd judged her mother so harshly, and now that she understood first-hand the way love could catch you off guard...

Hold on. Love?

She wiped a hand down her face. She wasn't ready for love. It hadn't gotten as far as love, had it?

The sound of the truck's motor was louder, and soon Nicole could see JT and his cousin driving down her grandmother's dirt road. Her heart thumped, and her hands got clammy. Nerves rioted in her stomach, and she debated running inside and hiding. She put her phone down next to her and wiped her damp hands across her jeans. She stood as Dante pulled up and shut off the engine. Her eyes widened when she spotted cuts and bruises along his face and neck as he got out of the passenger side of the truck. Her knees weakened, fear clutching her heart.

Guilt rushed through her. That was one question about the bond answered. It had been him she'd felt earlier. He'd been in danger, and instead of helping him, she'd turned off her phone. It was already starting. Love or not, she couldn't watch him be destroyed right before her eyes. Her chest ached with the decision she would make for the both of them. Still, seeing JT hurt, had her feet moving before her mind could stop her.

Nic rushed over. "Are you okay?"

He didn't move from the door. "You didn't answer your phone."

"A lot was going on today. I'm sorry."

"I found out something about your aunt today." He leaned his shoulder against the truck door, his eyes studying her face.

She wanted to go to him. The need to care for him had her hands shaking. She raised her hand to cup his cheek. "What happened to you?"

"Got into some shit on a run." He moved his head to avoid her hand.

If she touched him, all the resolve he'd built up on the way over would crumble. He wasn't in the business of begging. And just the sight of her had him near that. His wolf was whining, urging him to go to her, to deepen their bond. He intentionally blocked out the tumultuous feelings coming from her end of the mating bond. His animal would never let him leave otherwise.

She sighed. "Which aunt?"

"Your aunt Rebecca."

They both looked up as Ness came out the front door.

"What's going on?" Ness asked.

Nic cleared her throat. "JT said he had something about Aunt Becca."

"She sold, or rather, tried to sell the Fouche land to one of my clients, a practitioner, outside of Atlanta." JT pulled the paperwork out of his vest and passed it to them. "He said she did it in exchange for him settling some kind of debt she had."

"Oh my God." Nic snatched the papers from his hands impatiently, her eyes raking the text.

Ness was reading over her shoulder. "What the hell?"

"I saw her in Savannah gambling at an illegal joint run by some bears. According to them, she'd paid off the money she owed the place. It was the only reason he allowed her to play again."

"What the hell?" Nicole whispered. "Thank you, JT. I know you didn't have to—"

"I thought you'd want to know." JT turned to open the truck door.

Ness shared a look with Nicole. She took the pages and rolled them up. "I'll take this inside and call Cellus. You handle this."

There was nothing to handle as far as he was concerned. Nicole didn't want anything serious with him, and his wolf would no longer accept less than that. Hell, even the man. He wanted to blame it all on his wolf, but Nicole had gotten under his skin. An ache he couldn't assuage. He sighed.

She stepped closer to him. "JT, I'm sorry. We should talk."

He cocked his head and waited on her to speak.

"I've been struggling with the idea of this," she started. "I don't want my family's curse to touch you—"

"Don't use that excuse to push me away!" He snapped. "My job is dangerous, Nicole. The shit I choose to do is my choice and has nothing to do with your family curse. Has it occurred to you that the world doesn't revolve around the Fouches?"

They stared each other down, and she took a step back in the face of his anger. It pissed him off more. Did she think he'd hurt her? Maybe the crux of it all was that she didn't trust him. Women wanted security, and Lord knew it wasn't something he could guarantee with his job. It could be that she didn't want him, and if that were the case... He sucked in a sharp breath at the thought.

"If you don't want to be with me, then fine. Let it be that. Don't be bringing no funky ass curse into it."

"It's not safe, JT," she whispered.

His breath stalled, and pain that had nothing to do with his wounds made his body tremble. She was giving up on them. There was nothing else to be said. JT shook his head and opened the truck door. He hid a wince as he climbed up into the cab.

Despite her words, he still expected her to try and stop him. To put up some resistance to him leaving, but she said nothing, just stood and watched him. He shook his head and inclined his head at Dante to take off. He wouldn't beg.

"Cuz," Dante started.

"Don't, Te. Just drop me off at home."

The parking lot of Lore was packed, and JT was not in the mood. Dante drove the truck around the back and let him out.

"Make sure you have someone take care of those wounds," he ordered.

Dante gave him a pained smirk. "Shit, you worse than me."

JT grunted because that was the damned truth. His body ached, along with his heart as he climbed the stairs to his apartment. He sighed and leaned his forehead on his front door, the scents from within finally reaching him through his distraction.

"Fuck," he whispered.

He opened the door, and his parents were both sitting on his sofa, Valarie's face suffused with worry, while his Pops kept a comforting arm around her shoulder.

His mother jumped up first. "We heard what happened at Jedidiah."

She hissed as she got closer, her eyes widening in surprise. He knew she'd caught the stench of the ghast on him. That was a relief, in a way. It would buy him a little time before his mother realized that he'd bonded with Nicole. Though he knew with the unrest between them, they hadn't reached the stage of bonding where their scents had melded.

"I'm fine, mama." JT peeled off his leathers and hissed as the air brushed against the wounds his wolf had not got around to healing yet.

"My ass," Valarie said, rushing to his side. Her hands trembled as she helped him out of his shirt and led him to the recliner in his small living room. "I'll get something to speed these along."

His father waited until his wife left the room before he spoke.

"I'm proud of you, JT. Defeating a practitioner that powerful is gonna add to the legend of this pack."

"Really Will, pack business when our son is sitting there on his last leg?" Valarie snapped.

Last leg?

He hid his laugh with a cough and regretted it when the muscles of his abdomen pulled.

"Lord, you're so dramatic, woman. One good shift, and the boy'll be fine." Will rolled his eyes and settled back on the sofa with his arms crossed over his chest.

His mother scoffed and sighed, his dusty first aid kit useless in her hand. She tucked her lips in, refusing to concede Will's point.

"Up, Jeremiah, and into the shower. Wash off all that blood and let me see what's what," his mother ordered instead.

JT grimaced as he stood to do her bidding. Arguing with her was useless. He shed his pants once he'd closed his bedroom door, heading for the bathroom. He winced as he got a glimpse of himself in the mirror on his dresser. He looked like shit, the evidence of the brutal battle he'd fought all over his face and shoulders. Bruises colored his eyes and cheekbones, and several healing scrapes scored his shoulders and chest. The shifter and ghast Jed had set on him, and Dante had damn near done the job they'd been ordered to do.

"And don't be in there lollygagging," Valarie called out.

JT sighed. It was going to be an even longer night than he'd planned.

Chapter Thirty-One

"Do you think they'll show up?"

Nic rolled her eyes at Audrey's question. If their Uncle and his wife didn't show up, she was going over there and dragging their ass back to Grandmother's house. She, Ness, and Audrey were in the living room waiting on everyone to arrive for the family meeting. It was a risk confronting Aunt Becca with everyone around, but what other choice did they have? She and her cousins were all in agreement that no one was calling the police. So all that was left was figuring out how to take care of it as a family.

They all tensed as a car pulled into the yard. Ness rushed to the front window.

"It's Cellus and Bev," Ness told them, closing the curtain back.

But, when the door opened, Aunt Shelby and Damian were with them. Their faces were solemn as they came in. Audrey moved over on the sofa to make room for Beverly and their Aunt Shelby.

"Did he agree to come?" Cellus asked, settling into one of the armchairs adjacent to the sofa.

Audrey nodded. "He said he would. I was just asking them if they thought he would actually show up."

"Nicole, can you explain what is going on? Marcellus just said it was important." Aunt Shelby raked them all with a worried look.

Nic twisted her hands together. "JT came over earlier. He said that Aunt Becca had sold the Fouche land in exchange for some debts she had."

Aunt Shelby sucked in a sharp breath. "That's not possible."

"It's certainly not legal," Bev said, sitting forward. "Where is this paperwork?"

Ness handed it over, and Bev unrolled it, her eyes skimming over it. They were quiet as she read over the contract.

"I don't..." Bev sighed. "It's a practitioner's contract? What the shit?"

"Practitioner?" Shelby snatched the paper from Bev. "Lord have mercy. She was dealing with Jedidiah? Ain't no way this is happening."

"You know who that is?" Nic asked, surprised.

"He's been after the power on this land for years. Mama promised him she'd kill him if he came back to try again." Shelby told them.

"JT took care of that," Ness chimed in.

Nic whipped to her cousin. "He did what?"

"That's why he was beat up to hell and back. Jed put a contract on JT. According to Dante, if JT were around, Jedidiah wouldn't have been able to keep the land." Ness said it all matter of factly.

"When in the hell did you learn all of this?" Nic asked, shook.

She wanted more than anything to go to JT, to nurse him back to health. He'd fought on their behalf? She felt like a coward for letting him go last night.

"We have a pact with the wolves. Of course, Jeremiah wouldn't let an outsider come in here and take our land," Shelby handed the papers back to Bev.

"Hold on. Wait, what?" Nic pressed a hand to her forehead.

"Everyone knows that, Nic," Damian added. "The Taylor wolves protect this whole town. He and Grandmother were in business together."

Nicole sat down on the ottoman next to Marcellus. How in the hell hadn't she known that? There was so much about this town that she didn't know and didn't understand. JT was tied all up and through her family. Was that why he was so flippant about their family's curse?

"Lord, Grandmother was doing business with a motorcycle gang? No wonder the police ain't doing shit," Audrey murmured.

"They're here," Ness whispered from the window.

Nic took a deep breath and pushed aside her problems with JT. Nerves had her stomach tossing and turning. This could go wrong in so many different ways. Everyone was silent, the tension taut enough that anything was liable to make it snap. She swallowed, her throat dry and tight. Her uncle Brandon and Aunt Becca came through the door, and both of them frowned at the sight of everyone.

"Good evening, y'all," Brandon greeted, easing Becca into the only vacant chair in the living room.

"You got some explaining to do, Rebecca," Shelby snapped.

Becca looked around the room with wide eyes, "Me? What did I do?"

Damian put a restraining hand on his mother's shoulder, standing behind her. Beverly passed the papers over to her husband, and Marcellus handed them to Uncle Brandon.

"These papers are proof that Aunt Becca tried to sell the Fouche land," Marcellus informed him.

Brandon scoffed and looked down at the papers. "Becca has no claim over this land. There is no legal way she could sell it."

"Which is why she didn't do it legally," Nic said.

Brandon frowned over the paperwork. "This is foolishness. A witch or sorcerer, whatever the hell they call themselves. Becca doesn't believe in that mess Mama and Shelby are tied up in."

"Excuse the hell outta you," Shelby hissed.

"Mama," Cellus warned. He turned back to Uncle Brandon. "Regardless of what you believe, this Jedidiah believed he had rights to this land."

"Is that why you called this ridiculous family meeting? To level accusations at me?" Becca waved her hand.

"This is nonsense," Brandon said, tossing the papers on the coffee table.

"We also found out that she was in Savannah gambling. It's making me think that it wasn't you who stole the money, Uncle Brandon." Nic crossed her arms over her chest and studied them both. "Aunt Becca, don't you have access to the accounts as his personal assistant?"

Becca blanched, and her Uncle Brandon looked genuinely surprised. It only took him seconds to clear his countenance.

"Why do you keep bringing up the money? I paid mama back," Brandon insisted.

"Okay, but now we're finding out that your wife's debts were paid off by someone trying to swindle our family land. You can see how we'd be concerned," Damian spoke up.

"It seems to me that the money you used to pay back Grandmother came from some unscrupulous person, sorcerer or not." Nic inputted.

"I'm retiring. This won't be an issue any longer," Brandon hastened to assure them.

"But she's still gambling, Uncle Brandon," Audrey said, exasperated. "What if we can't stop the next person who comes after this family through her?"

Brandon stood from the chair's arm and stared down at his wife. "You're still gambling?"

"Brandon." Becca reached out to grab his arm. "Let me explain."

He shook off her hand. "You promised."

"I'm sorry," Becca whispered, her eyes filling.

"You swore it would be the last time. I covered for you. My last words to my mother were angry because I was defending you," he hissed and moved from her.

"I tried, I swear!" Becca cried.

Like a sack of bricks, a realization hit Nicole. She gasped and stood. "Grandmother would've kept track of Jedidiah if he was a real threat," she said softly, puzzling through the horrid thoughts working their way into her head.

"She absolutely kept watch on what Jedidiah was doing," Shelby assured her.

"Plus, someone who has been trying to best Grandmother wouldn't have turned down the chance to gloat about what he'd done," Nic murmured as she paced.

"Oh God," Shelby whispered. "Are you thinking..."

Nic paced back to her Aunt Becca. "Grandmother knew what you'd done."

Becca looked faint, her face ashen as she turned to her husband.

"No," Brandon said softly.

"It was an accident, Brandon. You have to believe me," Becca stood and scurried to her husband's side.

Brandon reached out for the wall, his knees going weak. Marcellus was there to catch him and guide him into a chair. Shelby started crying, and Damian leaned down, holding his mother from behind.

"You killed our Grandmother?" Audrey asked, her body swaying.

Beverly grabbed Audrey, and they clung together.

Becca lowered her head, sobs wracking her body. She looked up, tears streaming down her face. "She called me over to tell me what she'd found out. Patsy was going to turn me in. I begged her to think about what it would do to all of y'all, but she wouldn't change her mind. I just...I just wanted her to put down the phone."

"You killed my mother!" Aunt Shelby raised from the sofa faster than Damian could stop her.

The slap she landed on Becca's cheek rang out in the room. The ensuing slaps and punches were rapid-fire before Marcellus could grab her. Shelby fought against her son, trying to reach for Becca. Power swelled in the room, and Nic's puma responded, filling her body with magic. Her body trembled as Aunt Shelby's anger roiled across them all. Nicole took deep, shaky breaths battling the power electrifying her skin.

"You will pay for this. I will spend the rest of my life making sure that you do," Shelby swore as Marcellus handed her off to his brother.

Damian dragged their mother into the kitchen, her wails still reaching them. Nic's throat tightened with unshed tears and hurt for her family. It took long moments of tense silence before Shelby's power dissipated, freeing them all from the hold it had over them.

"She has to go," Marcellus demanded, leveling a hard stare at their aunt. His voice was shaky from the residual power in the room.

"No," Becca whispered. "Please."

"I'll go with you, Cellus," Bev said quietly, her hand going to her husband's chest. "I can call ahead to the station and let them know."

"Brandon, please. Don't let them do this to me...to us." Becca pleaded.

Brandon was dazed, his stare blank and straight ahead. Nic touched his arm. Her magic was heightened from her aunt's outburst, so it rushed forward, and his emotions swamped her. She could feel his heartbreak; there was guilt, devastation, and anger, a whole quagmire of it roiling around her uncle. Her eyes welled with the strength of it.

"What am I supposed to do?" he whispered.

"I'm so sorry, Uncle Brandon," Nic told him softly.

He shuddered, tears leaking from his eyes. "I'll have to go to the station with her. She's my wife. I've taken care of her all our lives."

Nic's heart shattered with his pain. She shared a helpless look with Ness, who had a crying Audrey clutched tight. Ness's fury reached Nic, and it was something she understood and shared with her cousin.

"Let's go, Uncle Brandon." Marcellus's voice was tired, his eyes red from the tears he held back.

Nic stood and backed away so their uncle could stand. He aged right before her eyes, lines etched on his face as grief weighed down his shoulders. The tears that had clogged her throat finally broke through, and Nicole let out a shuddering breath. What would this do to her family?

Chapter Thirty-Two

It had been two weeks since he'd left Nicole at her grandmother's house, and JT felt every second of the separation. His wolf was on his last god-damned nerves, and his disposition was less than hospitable. And yet, whether it be stubbornness or spite, he was in the club, pretending as though his wolf wasn't shredding his insides mourning their mate.

Dante racked up the pool balls and eyed him from across the table. "You good, Cuz?"

"Ask me again, and I'm liable to rock your shit, Dante." JT groused, chalking the tip of his pool stick.

"Just saying. You been growling for the past two hours, and I know I can't be the only one riled by your wolf," Dante commented, rubbing at his chest.

"You ain't the only one," Will called out as the front door of the club slammed. His father sauntered over to them.

JT held back the curses on the tip of his tongue.

"Luckily for you, ain't nobody in this bitch. Otherwise, somebody'd be fighting." Will settled into one of the stools at the table next to them.

"Pops," JT greeted his father reluctantly.

He'd planned to stew for a few more days yet. If Will was showing up at the bar in the middle of the day, it meant his parents had other ideas. Will nodded his head towards the back, and Dante got the message. His cousin stored his pool stick and left the two of them alone.

"You wanna talk about it?"

JT lined up the cue ball and broke. "I don't, Pops."

His father didn't say anything else, just watched him bang the balls around the table for a few minutes. JT growled, knowing the male wouldn't leave until he'd said his piece. He put the stick down and sat next to his father. He poured two fingers of the Bourbon he and Dante had been sipping from and gave it to his father.

"There's nothing to talk about, Pops. She letting that curse shit get in her head and ain't nothing I can do about it."

Will sipped at his drink and watched his son, a smirk on his face. "If you wanted an easy woman, son, you should've left them Fouches alone."

"I set myself up, I know." JT sighed.

"Taylors are stubborn as fuck. I chased your mama damn near across every piece of Alabama before she would admit that she was mine. Our wolves don't do weak women." His father smiled into his glass and took another sip. "I'd do that shit all over again for the privilege to touch your mama, though."

"I don't beg." JT grabbed the bottle and took it to the head.

"You spoiled like shit is what you is. All them females got your head big because you ain't had to do nothing to get nor keep 'em." Will shook his head. "If you ain't willing to work for your mate, then you don't deserve her."

JT slapped the bottle down. "Pops, what you want me to do? I damn near laid my shit out for her to stomp on, and she still said it wouldn't work."

"Damn near or did?"

JT frowned. "What?"

"Did you 'damn near' lay your heart out, or did you lay your heart out on the table?" Will asked, pouring himself some more bourbon.

"What's the difference?"

"JT, if you ain't tell the girl how you felt, then how the hell you expect her to choose you over whatever got her scared." His father shook his head.

"Fuck." JT took the bottle and drank again.

Had he told her how he felt? In the heat of the moment, he let his wolf go too far, but had he given her the words?

"Them Fouches different. They done been through some shit, JT. You seen first-hand some of it. Trust ain't something you'll get easy from Nicole."

"So you saying explaining the mating will get her to trust me?"

Will laughed. "Hell no. It's a start, but what you need to do is to convince her that, curse or no, every moment with you is better than the moments without you."

JT opened his mouth to refute that but closed it because...damn it. That was actually good advice.

They turned as the club's front door opened, letting in the mid-morning sun. JT squinted at the male who filled the doorway. The green khaki uniform he wore was pressed within an inch of its life, the gold star on his chest catching the sunlight.

"Ah hell," Will muttered, filling his glass again.

The male closed the door and looked around the dim club. He finally spotted them at the pool tables. His footsteps sounded loud in the empty place as he walked over. JT watched him until he stopped at the banister separating the pool tables from the rest of the club.

"Uncle Will," the male greeted, removing his hat.

His father eyed the deputy. "Nephew. Your mama know you over on this side of the tracks?"

JT snorted.

Trey turned his stern gaze to JT. "It's work-related."

JT crossed his arms over his chest and stared his cousin down. "Is that right?"

"Found a body out by the marsh," Trey stated.

"That's sad. How'd they die?" Will asked.

"Drowning," was Trey's answer.

JT sipped from the bottle. "That's a damn shame. People gotta be careful in the marsh."

"Strange thing, though. He was also shot multiple times." Trey looked between them both, gauging their reaction.

"Probably made it hard to swim," Will said off-hand.

JT tightened his lips to hold back his smile.

"Would you know anything about that?" Trey addressed him.

"Swimming with a gunshot wound? Nah, I don't know shit about that." JT shrugged.

Trey sighed and tapped his hat against his leg. "I suppose it can't be traced back to you at all, either way."

"Especially since I ain't have nothing to do with it."

Trey stared, and JT held his gaze, having played this game with his cousin plenty of times before. Trey broke first as usual and looked away.

"Alright then." Trey acquiesced. "I heard they found some kind of necromancer dead north of here, right outside of Dalton. Do you know anything about that? Lot of talk around it."

"I can't do nothing about talk, Deputy Taylor. People will say anything." JT resumed drinking.

Trey nodded, "Probably got witnesses that put you hours away from there."

JT smirked. "Video evidence, even."

"Handy." Trey narrowed his eyes.

Silence fell between the three of them.

"Well, hey, you did your job and asked. That's what matters," Will said, holding his glass up in a salute, breaking the silence.

Trey snorted.

"What y'all doing with Becca Fouche? Heard she was the one that murdered Patsy," Will leaned on the table.

"She confessed. Ain't nothing to do but wait on the fancy lawyer her husband got her to negotiate a deal with the DA." Trey shrugged.

"Damn shame," Will said, shaking his head.

JT wondered how Nicole was doing with it all. He reached for his phone, his fingers tapping on the screen as he debated contacting her.

"Let me get on back to work, then," Trey said.

"Tell Aunt Trice we send our love," JT mocked.

All three of them knew Trey wouldn't tell his mother he was associating with 'that side of the Taylors'. His Aunt did everything in her power to keep her kids on the straight and narrow. That included keeping them away from her brothers and their heathen ways. She'd have a conniption if she knew her baby boy talked to them on the regular, both in and out of uniform.

"Will do. Later, Unc," Trey said, turning to leave. He stopped near the door. "Also, cousin, the county's bringing in some kind of paranormal task force. Got some new laws coming down on magic users and the stuff they've been using for their magic. Just something you might wanna consider as you go about your business."

"Noted, Deputy." JT saluted his cousin.

Trey shook his head and chuckled, leaving JT alone with his father again.

Will downed the last of the liquor in his glass. "I'm headed out with Earl. Just remember what I said, son, and stop all this sulking. You finna make us all look bad."

He slapped JT's back and walked out, leaving JT alone with his thoughts. He swirled the bourbon around the bottle, thinking back to his last conversation with Nic. He certainly hadn't told her his feelings then. His father had called him spoiled, and JT had to admit that there was some truth to that. Women had always been easy for him, and when they weren't, he'd had no problems putting them to the side for those that were.

How could he get past her fear of the curse? Was it the only reason she held back from him? Could it be as simple as him confessing his feelings for her to give them a chance? He shook his head, he didn't think so, but he was willing to try anything at this point.

Chapter Thirty-Three

The house was silent, the rest of her cousins slept upstairs, but Nicole had beat the sun awake. Even now, the soft orange rays were seeping beneath the curtains over the windows in her grandmother's workshop. Despite the new day's dawning, past days weighed down the whole house. The energy was heavy, and after a week of letting the unease hold her, she was done with that. Sulking was not something she ever allowed for herself, not when others had it so much worse than her.

It was time to clean—first, the energy and then the physical. Nic rooted around her grandmother's cabinets until she found what she was looking for. Gathering the herbs and the bundle of twine, she set them on the table, smiling as the piney smell of the juniper rose and filled the room. She added lavender and wound the twine around them, humming as she did.

She spied the small, worn wooden bowl on top of a short bookshelf. Grabbing it, she lit the herb and waved her hand over it until all that remained was a tiny ember.

Nicole closed her eyes as smoke drifted from the herb bundle in her hand. She inhaled the scent and rolled her shoulders a few times to ease the tension tightening them for the past week.

"Earth, water, fire and air...."

"Within me, all things are there," Ness finished from the doorway.

Nic opened her eyes and smiled. "You remember?"

"How many times had Grandmother sat us in the middle of the floor, 'legs crossed, eyes closed'—"

"'And yo' mind on Spirit,'" Audrey inserted as she joined them in the study.

They shared a laugh.

Nic sighed and willed the lump in her throat away. "My God, I miss her."

"I miss those days," Audrey said softly. "Everything seemed possible."

"You're smudging?" Ness asked.

"I can't take it anymore. I'm going to clear the energy, and then we're cleaning the house," Nic told them.

Audrey nodded. "Perfect. I'll make some coffee, and by the time you're done, I'll be ready."

Nic nodded and left the room, and started her prayers. She went from room to room, hitting every corner, every doorway, and window, dispelling the negative energy that had coalesced in the house. She lost herself in the ritual, clearing her mind of everything. Both upstairs and downstairs, she covered the whole house.

True to her word, by the time Nic had come downstairs again, Audrey had started on the kitchen. The three of them weren't messy by any stretch of the imagination, so cleaning wouldn't take them long. The process, though, that was the most important part— sweeping away the dust and physically cleaning away that which bogged down the house. Nicole was sweating by the time they'd finished, but it was well worth it. The house felt lighter, and with it, her thoughts became clearer. As she entered her bedroom to take a shower, her mind went to JT and the fact that she hadn't talked to him in two weeks.

A part of her wanted to call him. With everything happening with their Aunt Becca, the turning over of the company, she would've loved to be able to talk to him about that. He had a way of boiling things down to their simplest denominator and making them easier to digest. It had been hard to watch her aunt go through the wheels of the justice system. Even though they'd have someone to 'pay' for their grandmother's murder, it didn't bring Patsy back. And it certainly hadn't made the family feel any better.

They should've come out on the other side divided, but her family had pulled together. They'd rallied around Uncle Brandon, even as Aunt Shelby spat Becca's name. Damian was helping Audrey at the brewery, and she and Ness were making arrangements to move their lives to Georgia. To that end, she'd been spending more time with her Aunt Shelby, learning from her. Not only had she been learning how to hone the magic she had inherited, her aunt had been taking her around the town to meet people.

According to Aunt Shelby, an essential part of being a Fouche was being a part of the community. It rooted their magic and reminded them of what was at stake. She'd gone to Aunt Shelby's yoga classes, went grocery shopping with her, and even somewhat begrudgingly woke up for church the last two Sundays. She wouldn't be doing that often, though, because she liked her weekend sleep-ins. She'd been doing everything she could do to meld and make herself a part of this new community.

Now, Nic just needed to figure out what she wanted to do about JT. He didn't believe her family's curse applied to him. She shook her head at the arrogance. It was one thing she loved about him, but damn if it didn't...

She paused in the act of pulling off her shirt. Love. It was one of the many things she loved about JT. She sat down hard on the bed and took a shuddering breath. She loved him. Despite all the walls she'd built around her heart, he'd managed to push his way through.

Her heartbeat thundered in her chest, and the cold fingers of panic gripped her throat. If she never saw him again, would that prevent the curse from working on him? Or was it a done deal? He said his job was already dangerous, which was scary for her for several reasons. Nicole could lose him from either the curse or the danger surrounding his job. She didn't win in either of those scenarios.

She thought back to her mother's words.

If she were already destined to lose him, why deprive herself of the love they could enjoy in the meantime? How many years would she have with him? Could anyone in a relationship answer that question with certainty? Curse or not, life was not promised, and forever love was never guaranteed, so why would she waste the time they could have? Mating with a shifter was forever, according to her Aunt Shelby. It was a close to a guarantee as anyone could have, and she was fucking it up by letting fear rule her.

That ended today.

Chapter Thirty-Four

At some point, JT had to admit that sulking wasn't working. Well, he didn't think of it as sulking, and he'd snapped on the last person to call it that. Now his aunt was mad at him. If he had to call it something, he'd prefer brooding. That was a better word. It had been three weeks since he'd left Nic's side, and he longed to see her. He'd been on the road back and forth the whole time. With the mood his wolf was in, he'd cemented the reputation the Taylor wolves had along the way. His lousy mood would pay off, at least in that. His pack mates, on the other hand... Dante had booted him from the clubhouse and told him not to come back until he'd calmed down.

Now, he was outside in his wolf form, currently eating on a deer he'd run down an hour ago. Giving his animal control was the only thing keeping the beast in a semi-decent mood. His wolf was restless and broody, or was that the man? He growled and tore into the deer.

He looked up when he felt someone watching him. His mother stood a few feet from him, her hands on her hips.

"Why you at my back door playing with your food?"

He cut his eyes up at her but continued to gnaw on the deer he'd dragged to the edge of the woods. Nowhere near Valerie's back door. By the time she told her sisters-in-law the story, JT will have been tearing into a live deer in the middle of her living room. The woman loved to exaggerate.

She sighed. "Jeremiah, I ain't in the mood for your pouting, so if you want to talk, I'll be in the house." She turned around and left him.

Pouting? See...exaggerating.

Growling, he dragged the deer farther into the woods away from her house so it wouldn't draw scavenger animals close to her garden and shifted back. He used the hose in her backyard to clean up. Once done, he walked inside, pulling on one of the robes his mother kept on a hook near the back door. Valerie shook her head at him and went back to watching tv as he passed her on the way to find clothes.

He took a long hot shower and joined her on the sofa nearly an hour later. She side-eyed him but didn't say anything. He hid his smile because he knew she wouldn't be able to keep from butting into his business long. He laid his head on her lap and turned towards the TV and whatever murder show she was watching.

Valerie sighed and tapped the top of his head. Her wolf rose, brushing across his cantankerous animal, and soothing them both. JT released a sigh and closed his eyes as the wolf finally settled within him. God, he loved his mama.

"Don't let your daddy catch you laying in my lap. You know he already called you spoiled."

He grunted. "He'll be alright."

"Your Auntie Ruth called and said you were slapping Pooh around." There was no censure in her tone.

"Pooh ol' soft ass," he murmured.

"Still ain't talk to Nicole?" She finally got around to what she wanted to know.

He debated his next words. The Fouche curse could be a touchy subject. His mother had already warned him about it and Nicole. He was almost sure that Valerie wasn't at all sad over the fact that he and Nic weren't talking.

"I saw her at the minute market a couple of days ago, had the nicest manners." That was his mother's way of calling her bougie.

"She called it off, said we weren't a good idea." He shrugged.

She rubbed his head and sighed. "I'm sorry, baby, but—"

"Don't, mama." He cut her off. He already knew her thoughts on the matter.

"I could smell your scent all over her, so I guess I don't need to ask how your wolf feels about her."

"She's ours."

Valerie sucked her teeth. "I guess doing stuff the easy way has never occurred to you or that rabid animal you share your body with."

He laughed outright. "Now my wolf is rabid. Wow, mama, just say you don't want me to date a Fouche. No call to insult my animal."

"I just want my son safe. I don't have anything against the girl personally."

He sat up and faced his mother. Her forehead was creased in worry, her eyes watering. JT sighed.

"Mama."

She held up a hand. "I'm fine. You will do what you want, Jeremiah. You been that way your whole life. Please, just be careful."

He grabbed her into a tight hug. "I'm always careful, mama."

She nodded and dropped it. Unless he could find a way to get Nicole to talk to him, her tears were premature, but he kept that to himself.

"You don't have womanly advice for me on how to get her back?" He teased.

She growled and pinched his arm. "You get on my nerves." She turned her gaze to the TV for a few beats and then sighed.

"The bonding comes in three steps. I'm sure your daddy done went over it with you. The first step is there before you even bite your mate. That initial obsession you had with Nicole was that. Then comes your bite; it intertwines your mind and soul. That part is the easiest. It's just plain ol' biology. The last part, the part you're struggling with, only comes when there is complete trust between mates." She cupped his cheek. "Tell her how you feel, Jeremiah. Don't make it more complicated than that."

She was right. All of it had been needlessly complicated. His animal was out of patience with him, and he didn't want to go another day without her.

"Trust is hard for her. She has the same worries you do," he told her.

She nodded. "That makes me like her more."

"So, how do I gain her trust?"

Valerie shrugged. "The Fouches, for all their power and magic, lack the one thing most people need, and that is security. So much turmoil in that family from way back. Show Nicole different. Be that for her, and the trust will come."

JT absorbed his mother's words and understood, for the first time, what he could do to win Nicole over. It was time to go to her.

Nicole took a deep breath and knocked on JT's apartment door. She turned and looked back at her cousins waiting at the bottom of the stairs. Ness shrugged, and Audrey's smile was encouraging, if a little sympathetic. She tried again, and when he didn't answer, she went down to the bottom of the stairs.

"What do you want to do?" Ness asked her.

She'd had her speech planned, all the words she'd been afraid to say to him carefully written out, and now she was deflated. Could she work up the courage again to say what she needed to?

"No matter," she said aloud.

She went to her waiting jeep and pulled out the jugs of purified water as well as the red brick dust. She'd scoured her grandmother's journals for something she could do to protect JT better. The spell was a simple but supposedly effective one. She'd run it by Aunt Shelby to be on the safe side and had gotten the okay. Protecting JT's home was but one step in her plan. Ness grabbed the empty bucket and brushes before Nic could attempt to balance it all.

"We'll do it with you," Audrey said quietly as Nic backed out of the open hatch. "Maybe our combined magic will help." She offered.

Nic's throat tightened, and she took a deep, shuddering breath. She wasn't alone anymore. She would have to get used to that.

"Thank you," she whispered, her eyes burning with unshed tears.

Ness nodded, and they started the process. Nic mixed the red brick dust into the water and set her intentions as she weaved her power into the mixture. She took another deep breath and nodded to her cousins. Ness and Audrey pushed their hands into the red water, and their lips moved as they each infused their power into it. Combining the power of the three of them would give the spell extra weight. Her chest tightened in gratitude for her cousins. They backed away, and Nicole grabbed the bucket and headed back to JT's stairs.

She started at the bottom and set about scrubbing the stairs one at a time with the mixture, praying as she went up each one. She'd reached the middle step when she felt him. The spot on her neck where JT had bitten her warmed, and her body shuddered as longing filled her, tightening her chest. She'd missed him. Every single day since she'd cut him off, she'd missed him. Just being in the same space as him loosened her muscles and lowered the anxiety that had ridden her for the past three weeks despite everything she did to combat it.

Even with his presence, she didn't stop what she was doing. She was nearly done, and now more than ever, wanted it done. She needed him protected from the curse that would aim his way now that she'd accepted their bonding. She'd taken the time away from him thinking, meditating, and nothing she did had removed her need for him. The tears she'd been fighting slid from the corners of her eyes.

"Nic," JT called her name softly.

She didn't stop scrubbing, instead moving faster, her throat tightening. Where were all the words she'd practiced? She went back to her chants, carrying the bucket up another step. She asked her ancestors to aid in his protection and begged God to cover him. Tears tracked down her cheeks, and fear had her muscles clenched tight.

She couldn't lose him.

"Nicole," JT said louder, his hand on her shoulder. "Love," he whispered, stooping next to her.

"I have to finish."

She moved up another step, just three more to go. She pushed his presence out of her mind and continued her prayer, her lips moving rapid-fire as she repeated the spell. Her power swelled, the magic surrounding her. She felt his wolf reach out to her, the heat from the animal's magic intertwining within hers. If she wanted, she could take control of the animal. She felt in on the edges of her magic, beckoning.

"What is she doing?" JT's voice pierced her concentration, but she pushed it out again.

"Adding protection to your place," Audrey told him.

One more step to go.

She scrubbed harder, her arms aching. JT didn't go back down the stairs, instead standing close to her as she finished. She felt the heat of him at her back. Once she was done, she breathed a sigh of relief and sat on the top step. Water soaked through her jeans.

"You say you don't want anything to do with me, and yet I find you here, doing this." He didn't pose it as a question, so she didn't say anything.

"I love you, Nicole," he said, and her heart caught.

It was the first time he'd said it aloud, but in her heart, she'd known that.

"I don't want to lose you," she whispered.

"So we don't even get a chance?"

"I'm going into this with my heart pre-broken." She said, and he chuckled.

"Fouche," he sighed. He kissed the top of her head and pulled her into his lap. "Hands down, you gotta be the most pessimistic person I've ever met."

His wolf reached out to her, and she allowed their power to mingle, to reacquaint. He shuddered and held her tighter.

"You're not worried about the curse?"

"Not while I'm holding you," was his answer, and that just...

Nic buried her face into the crook of his shoulder. She took a deep breath inhaling his scent. She moved his shirt aside so she could rest her cheek against his bare skin, her cat demanding it.

"If you're willing to risk it, I can too," she whispered.

He didn't say anything, just rubbed her back. They sat on the step as the sun dipped below the horizon. Audrey and Ness had long left with a promise to call and check on them later.

"The full moon is in a couple of days," he said suddenly.

She lifted her head and frowned. "Okay?"

He put his hand against her heart. "I can feel your cat rising. You don't feel her?"

She sighed. "Lately, I've been feeling her more. But with the curse, I don't know that the cat is ever really mine to control like the way your wolf is."

"Have any of you tried to break the curse?"

"I think the three of us are going to try."

He nodded. "Then let's dead talking about it for now. I'm with you until the end, Nic, but you gotta meet me halfway."

She cupped his cheek and brought his lips down to hers. "I'm all in."

Their lips met, and the kiss they shared was ravenous, both of them starving for the touch of the other. His wolf reached for her, and her cat responded, their magic comingling filling them. Nic gripped his shoulders as a riot of emotions crashed over her. His worry and love were there, as well as a deep yearning that had her chest clenching. Being back in his arms drove home how integral he'd become to her happiness. She'd hadn't been necessarily unhappy while they'd been apart, but the feeling coursing through her now with his presence made a mockery of any contentedness she'd thought she'd had. In his presence, even her power had a brighter feel to it.

For however many moments they got, being with him was well worth it.

Before he even opened his eyes, JT reached for Nicole. It wasn't the first time he'd done it since they'd fallen asleep last night, and every time she'd been there, her body arching into his arms. This morning, though, her side of the bed was empty. For a brief moment, he panicked. Was it like all the times when she left in the morning insistent that she couldn't spend the night? Before he could fully leap to conclusions, the smells of breakfast filtered into his bedroom. He breathed a sigh of relief and opened his eyes.

He stretched his body, happy for every ache. Though he'd not gotten many hours of sleep, the sleep that he did get was some of the best he'd had in a while. He rolled over and shook his head. He was getting soft. A woman staying the night would have never elicited this type of excitement before. Funny how the tables had turned. He made the bed and then went through his morning routine. He pulled on pair of jeans when he was done in the bathroom and walked out to his living room. Nicole was at the stove, humming and, from its smell, cooking bacon.

She smiled at him as he entered the kitchen. He sidled behind her, pulling her into his arms and licking across his mating mark. Her relaxed mood filtered to him through their tighter bond. His wolf lazily moved through his body before settling. Contentment filled him, along with new and heady power. He closed his eyes and examined the magic. Did she know their mating would gift him with the extra power? He'd noticed it when he'd battled Jedidiah, but this was more. Was it because she finally had given in to the mating? Pushing it aside for later, he slid his hand under her sleep shirt. He nibbled across her shoulder and tensed as he looked across the room. Three large suitcases were taking up space next to the front door.

"I need clothes if I plan on staying here," she said off-handed, but she stilled, waiting on his reaction.

"So you staying in Georgia, then?"

She turned the burner off and turned to face him. "Yes." She wound her arms around his neck, and her eyes traced his face. "A part of me is still scared to make any permanent type plans."

"I can understand that, but this..." he traced his mark with a finger. "This is permanent."

She shuddered as he retraced it, her eyelids lowering. Her scent deepened, her arousal rising. He pulled her tighter into his body, his erection pushing against her stomach. He sucked on his mark again, laving it with his tongue. Her head lolled back, and she scraped her nails across his back.

"We shouldn't be starting anything. I got work today."

He growled and bit down on her neck. A blush worked through her, heating her skin beneath his hands.

"You brought your laptop with you, didn't you?"

She moaned as he gripped her neck. "Hell no. I left it at Grandmother's house. I knew I wouldn't get any work done if I brought it here. I can't be caught up in shenanigans during working hours."

He chuckled. "Shenanigans, huh?"

He turned their bodies until they faced the other counter, away from the hot stove. He lifted the sleep shirt she wore and passed his hands over her ass, cursing as lust tightened his body. He slid her panties to the side and hissed as he found her wet. He unbuckled his jeans with one hand and gripped his dick, guiding it to the place he wanted to be. He circled the opening of her sex, prolonging the torture.

"I won't have time to eat breakfast." Her protest was weak, especially since she widened her stance to give him more space.

"You'll be alright," he said softly, closing his eyes as he slid home.

Fuck, the way her heated walls clamped down on him. The woman was incredible and all his. She arched her back, taking him deeper and JT understood that he was so far gone where this woman was concerned. He pulled out slowly, enjoying the heated slide. He pushed in again, harder this time, entranced with the way her ass shook with the motion. She moaned and met his strokes.

"Quit playing with me. I got somewhere to be," she said hoarsely, swiveling her hips.

He didn't need further prodding than that. He dicked her down with deep strokes, enjoying Nic's every grunt and moan. It didn't take him long before the orgasm tightened his body. He reached around and rubbed on her clit until she was writhing against him, panting as she fought to reach her peak. He moved his finger faster, and she exploded, screaming. He powered into her until he followed her over the edge. She lowered the top of her body over the countertop and sighed.

"I'm gonna be late," she murmured, her voice content.

He smacked her ass and bit his lip as he watched it move. He pulled out reluctantly, wishing they had more time. "That's your fault. You knew what it was when your fine ass decided to stay."

She whipped around and narrowed her eyes at him. He laughed and gripped her chin, pulling her into a kiss before she cussed him out. She relaxed against him with a moan but then smacked his chest, separating from him.

"I gotta go." She rushed to one of her suitcases and wheeled it into his bedroom.

He hunted down a plastic container, sliding her food into it. He put it on top of her purse. He was cleaning the kitchen when she rushed back into the living room in a tank top and shorts that would haunt him all damn day. He skirted the counter and reached for her, but she danced out of his grip, sticking her tongue out.

"Aht-aht, stay your ass over there." She pointed at him, a broad smile on her face as she slid a thick sweater on over her shoulders. "I love you," she shouted, slamming his front door behind her.

He smiled, loving the sound of that. He looked at the time and figured there was probably work he could be doing in the bar. His eyes narrowed when he got to his room. They would need a bigger space. Her clothes were already scattered all over the place. From what he could see of the bathroom, she'd already claimed half the counter. If he asked Nicole, he was almost sure she would balk at the idea of getting a house with him. But, he wasn't worried; he was his father's son. Eventually, he'd wear her down. He had some property close to her grandmother's land where he could build them a place. She would be close to her cousins, and his pack mates would be able to come and go on the land without Ms. Patsy's wards all over the place.

His phone buzzed from his bedside table.

"Yeah."

"Got a run," Dante told him.

"Bet. Give me fifteen," he murmured.

He texted Nic and rushed through another shower. He was dressing in his leathers when she got back to him. Her message was a simple 'be careful'.

Yeah, Nic had brought changes to his life, but he could get used to his new life with her.

Epilogue

T*hree weeks later...*

Nicole slipped out of bed, careful not to wake JT sleeping soundly beside her. She wasn't sure what had woken her. She smiled down at her fine man, slipping a robe over her naked body. She probed the bond she had with him, loving that she had that option. Nicole had worked with him to strengthen it in the weeks since they'd fully bonded. It felt good being able to tell his moods and vice versa.

She headed for the kitchen, hoping a cup of tea would help her settle back to sleep. Her stomach fluttered with nervousness, and restless energy seemed to fill her body. She was filling the tea kettle when she felt another in the room. She looked up and yelped, seeing her grandmother was wandering around JT's living room, looking at his stuff.

Patsy turned at Nicole's scream and smiled.

"Grandmother," Nic whispered and rounded the kitchen island in a rush to get to her.

Patsy smiled and met her halfway. Nic stopped close to her, not sure if she'd be able to touch her grandmother, afraid even to try. She reached out a shaking hand anyway, and Patsy laughed.

"It's a dream, Nicole. Relax, my love."

Nicole cried out and grabbed her grandmother into a hug. "Oh my god, I miss you so much," she whispered.

Patsy pulled back and cupped her cheek. "I see you got the present I left for you."

Nic nodded. "I can't believe you left us the brewery."

Patsy chuckled and stepped back, "not that one, Bean." She nodded towards JT's bedroom.

Nic's eyes widened. "What do you mean?"

Patsy led her to the sofa, and they sat down together. "I looked up every spell and sigil I could for that boy."

Nic nodded. "He told me you helped him with half the work on his body."

Patsy sighed, "There is some powerful magic working against this family, and I wanted to give you all the chance I could."

"You couldn't have possibly known that JT and I would work out."

Patsy smiled, a secret brimming in her eyes. "That's not what I came to talk to you about."

"I'm just so glad that you came," Nicole said, gripping Patsy's hand tightly.

"I didn't have time to prepare the others for Vanessa and Audrey. You'll have to do that in my place."

"I don't... I'm not good enough." Nic protested.

Patsy put a hand on her leg. "You have my power and then some, Nicole. You can get good enough, though there isn't much time."

Her stomach dropped, and she searched her grandmother's face for clues as to what she was supposed to do.

"I've talked to Shelby. She'll help." Patsy assured her.

Nicole nodded, too overwhelmed to speak. What her grandmother was asking her to do would take way more training than she'd had with Aunt Shelby.

"Audrey will need you, Bean, so you gotta get after it, hear."

"Okay," she readily agreed, though she had no idea how she would accomplish the task.

"I love you. I'm proud of you. I know you've felt like an outsider, but it's time for you to forge your place in this family, in this town." She cupped Nicole's cheek.

Tears trailed down Nic's face as she nodded.

Patsy smiled and pulled her back into a hug. "Protect this family, Nicole."

Nic closed her eyes to savor her grandmother's closeness. She cursed when she opened her them and was back found herself back in bed, her face wet. She should've kept her eyes open just a bit more! She had so many more questions to ask her grandmother. She wanted more time! Nic certainly needed clarification on what Patsy wanted her to do. Prepare 'the others' for Audrey and Ness? What did that even mean? How would she even start? Her mind was spinning, and it took everything in her not to call Aunt Shelby and wake her with questions.

JT pulled her into his chest. His wolf brushed against her, soothing her grief and anxiety.

"You okay, love?" he whispered groggily.

"I will be," she said softly, curling her body into his.

She would be, she promised herself. She was a Fouche, and she would live up to her legacy come hell or high water.

Also available from Dria Andersen

Chasing Savannah

Hers to Call

Destiny Series

A Destiny Awakened

Destiny Revealed

Escaping Destiny

Haven Series

Haven

Soulbonded

Hellbound

The Hamilton Brothers

The Friend Contract

The Alpha Accord

About the Author

I am a full time photographer, and a mom of two. I've been writing my whole life, and after the birth of my first kid, I decided I couldn't very well bring up a fearless human without first trying the things that scared me. So, I wrote my first book, and then subsequently more.

I try to write stories I love to read: love stories that feature brown girls like me. Some of my stories feature gods and goddesses, and creatures I derived from old, African folk tales remixed and thrust into a modern world. Visit my website, www.driaandersen.com for more information on my other novels.

Join my newsletter!

www.ingramcontent.com/pod-product-compliance
Lightning Source LLC
Chambersburg PA
CBHW072005210726

48294CB00013B/1593